A KISS FROM A DRAGON LORD

KISS FROM A MONSTER SERIES
BOOK 3

CHARLOTTE SWAN

Cover Design by Haya, @hayaindesigns on Instagram

www.authorcharlotteswan.com

For those of us that dream of being a different kind of dragon rider...

1

ANWYN

I should've left this small town weeks ago.

It's always a risk staying too long in settlements like this one. It's easier to go unnoticed in larger towns; people hustling from their homes to work don't give someone like me a passing glance. In places like this, everyone knows each other. And a stranger taking up with the elderly woman in town, claiming to be her long-lost sister's granddaughter, arouses suspicion.

Mrs. Hitherbend is pushing her eightieth name day, and her memory has faded with time. Our paths crossed when I arrived by rowboat two months back. The town I was in previously had noticed me skimming some money from the mayor I was working for. He was a callous old man with wandering eyes and hands. He's lucky I just took his gold, not something he had a more permanent attachment to.

I had just enough coin to bribe a tradesman to take me as far as he could. That's how I ended up here. Mrs. Hitherbend saw me as soon as I docked and said I looked like her sister she hadn't seen in years. The lie I told her just spiraled from there until she gave me lodging in her house.

To be fair, I haven't completely exploited the woman. I've kept up with her washing, cooking her meals, and helping her with the tasks she's too frail to do. She's even given me a few gold coins for my work. Honestly, this is the best job I've had in a while.

I learned at a young age that we only have ourselves in this world. My parents died when I was young, leaving me penniless and with few options. I could either work myself to death as a servant to a noble family or sell my body to one of the brothels.

Instead, I decided to travel. Taking odd jobs in each town and creating aliases wherever I went in case the ones I took from tried to come after me. My crimes are minuscule compared to the ones I watched the wealthy commit on a daily basis. Each one of them using their wealth to circumvent justice or exploit those beneath them for sport.

After living so many years on the run, I began to see people as opportunities.

Life with Mrs. Hitherbend is monotonous, but an opportunity to acclimate smoothly to this new town nonetheless. It only took a short while for the townsfolk to accept me. The original plan was to stay through the winter, but as I was absorbed by the routine tasks, I let my guard slip. I had gotten too comfortable, and someone had finally taken note of me.

Mr. Wicksome.

A foul man, who I am now pouring tea for as he sits in Mrs. Hitherbend's kitchen. She absentmindedly prattles on about her chickens while his eyes rake over me. I was aware of his suspicions since I first arrived in this town. Two weeks ago, I overheard him talking to the blacksmith, saying there was something off about me and he was going to get to the bottom of it.

I should've left then, but the tradesman who brought me here before is returning tomorrow. I just have to make it through today, and tomorrow I will be on to my next destination. It's exhausting going from one place to the next but better to leave than be stuck with no way out.

"Ethel?" I cringe at the use of my fake name. "Could you fetch Mr. Wicksome and I some of those biscuits the Lees brought over last week? We rarely get visitors, and a man of your importance, Mr. Wicksome, deserves the best."

Forcing myself to smile, I nod and head into the kitchen.

Reaching up onto the top shelf, I pull down the jar of biscuits. The ceramic container sits heavy on the counter as I unscrew the top. My stomach sinks when I hear the wooden legs of a chair squeak against the stone floor.

There's heat at my back. I don't need to turn around to know who's standing there.

"I know your secret," Mr. Wicksome whispers near my ear, his hot breath making bile rise in my throat. "Anwyn."

Fuck.

I straighten my spine and turn towards him, meeting his beady eyes. His dark brown hair is graying at the temples; his skin is wrinkled and pot-marked. His clothes are made of quality wool but overly done, making him look less like a nobleman and more like a gaudy bird.

"I don't know what you're talking about."

He chuckles and shakes his head.

"You may be shocked to learn that I know a few people from that town you claim to be from. I gave them your name, and no one had heard of you." He steps closer, and I back up a step until the counter's edge presses into my back. "You haven't been very good at hiding your trail."

Mr. Wicksome curls a loose piece of my blonde hair around his finger.

"The butcher in that town recognized you from a coastal town down south. Only you went by Lila there. There is a shopkeeper down there who you worked for, but he knew you as Sophya in an eastern farming town. I was able to track down that farmer who remembers you staying with his family as a young girl named Anwyn."

My mouth goes dry; my palms begin to sweat.

"And in each of those towns, under each of those names, you are wanted for something, isn't that true?" My blood ices over.

"What do you want?" I spit out. The way his eyes linger on my chest tells me all I need to know. There are men like him everywhere. I've always been able to outsmart them before they got too far. My stomach curdles as I realize I may be out of moves. One word from him about where I'm located and all of my pasts may find me here.

"I am a powerful man, Anwyn. With the sway over this town to protect you if the people here found out what you truly are. They would not take too kindly to a thief and a liar deceiving them."

He drops the lock of my hair and steps back.

"What I want, Anwyn is for you to repay me for my silence."

"What would that entail?" Mr. Wicksome smirks as he walks back over to the table.

"My wife died a few years ago—"

"Yes," Mrs. Hitherbend interrupts, "what an unfortunate accident that was."

The room begins to spin and my knees begin to shake.

"Quite tragic, you are right. She was barren and left me without an heir. You appear `healthy enough to bare me a few. Therefore, I will take you as my wife and you will come and live with me as a part of my household."

"I—"

"How wonderful!" Mrs. Hitherbend cries, clapping her hands together. "I just got done telling Ethel she needs to find a good husband. One who will love and care for her when she's old and wrinkly like me."

I swallow as Mr. Wicksome grins, turning back towards the table. He digs around in his coat pocket until he produces a small bag of coins. Setting them down in front of Mrs. Hitherbend, he nods to her and then back to me.

"It is settled then. I will arrive at dawn with the priest, where I will take you as my wife." I just manage not to bare my teeth at him as he leers down my body again. "Make sure to get plenty of rest. You'll be needing it. I'm looking forward to you showing me just how grateful you are that I'm keeping your secret."

Reaching behind me, my fingers curl around the butter knife left out on the counter. The old metal grows hot in my hand. I should drive this dull blade into his neck, that would be another way to assure his silence.

However much I want to, I can't. Not as Mrs. Hitherbend leads him to the door and bids him farewell. I haven't moved from my spot in the small kitchen. My knees shake in time with my pounding heart.

"You are lucky, my dear," Mrs. Hitherbend says, sitting back down at the table. "Mr. Wicksome is a wealthy man who will take care of you."

"He's evil," I say.

"Nonsense child. Though I will miss your help around here, your place is at your husband's side. Giving him children. If only my sister were still alive, she'd be thrilled to hear about your good fortune."

Mrs. Hitherbend takes a sip of her tea that has long since gone cold. I let the knife clatter back onto the counter behind me. *Good fortune?* Any luck I may have had over these last years has finally decided to run out. Time is not on my side and one thing is certain: I can't stay in this village a moment longer.

Looking out the window, the cracks in the glass appearing like a cluster of cobwebs, I sigh deeply. I wish I had time to wait for the tradesman, but I can't risk it. The walls are closing in on me, and if I want to put enough distance between me and this town by morning, I'll need to set off now.

This village is the most remote place I've ever sought lodging. It's the last settlement for miles and is completely surrounded on each side by dense foliage. The townspeople all claim that *The Woods* are inhabited by nightmarish creatures who kill anyone who ventures inside. Tales to keep children from misbehaving if you ask me.

Besides, in my experience, humans are scarier than any creature this forest could conjure up.

Leaving Mrs. Hitherbend at the table, I quickly go to my room and pack the few items that I have in a worn leather bag. The only things to my name are a small bag of gold coins, an old book, and my mother's gold necklace. I need to travel light so I can make it through *The Woods* quickly. There has to be a town on the other side where I can seek shelter.

The leather on my boots is worn down, but it will hold for this journey. I cover my thin, gray wool dress with a dark cloak before slinging my bag across my shoulder. Quickly braiding back my hair, I walk into the kitchen and head for the door.

"Where are you going?" Mrs. Hitherbend asks.

My hand tightens on the doorknob as I dare a glance back over my shoulder. The deep wrinkles around her brown eyes stretch as she squints at me. Mr. Wicksome's dowry for me sits heavy on the table. I should take it, but I won't leave Mrs. Hitherbend with nothing.

Turning from the door, I march over to her as she leans back slightly in her chair. Scooping up the small bag of coins, I thrust it into her hands, closing her bony fingers around the purse.

"You don't have a sister," I say. Mrs. Hitherbend lets out a gasp. My hand tightens on hers, holding the coins. "A tradesman is coming in the morning. Buy passage on his ship and have him take you to the next town over. There is a doctor there who can help with your memory. Use this to pay for the treatment. Leave while Mr. Wicksome is busy searching for me."

"What do you mean—"

I don't hear the rest of her question. Moving quickly on my feet, I push through the door and onto the barren town street. No one is milling around; the dark rolling clouds overhead signal an impending storm. It's not ideal traveling weather, but that means no one is around to see me slip behind the house and walk fifty feet to the edge of the forest.

It's silent beyond the tree line. The sounds of twigs snapping and wildlife running through the leaves are absent. I chance one last look back at the village. A small pang of regret at the lies I told Mrs. Hitherbend threaten to weaken my resolve. Even after all these years of lying to survive, I'm not immune to the toll dishonesty can take on a person.

I shake myself from those thoughts. My guilty conscious isn't enough to make me marry a lecherous man like Mr. Wicksome. With a deep breath, I march forward, allowing myself to be swallowed up by the tall trees around me.

I s there anything more beautiful than sparkling gold?

Rubies and sapphires have their appeal, emeralds too, but nothing compares to the brilliant sparkle of gold. I can taste it in the air, its sharp metallic flavor coating my tongue and invading my lungs. The sound it makes as it clanks over my scales and shifts through my claws. Even now, as I dig my tail into the pile of gold coins I'm lying atop, their hard texture soothes me and makes me question what I could ever desire more than this.

When I was a human man, there were things I enjoyed. As the soon of a rich lord and a future lord myself, I partook in many luxuries. I enjoyed hunting with my father, large dinners filled with exotic dishes, and dancing until the early morning hours. All of those hobbies paled in comparison to the feeling of gold in my fingers.

From the first coin I received from my father on my tenth name's day to the large fortune he showed me would be mine upon his death, I began to crave it like no other. I found myself spending hours in the family vault, counting and cleaning each coin until they sparkled in the candle light. Betting with the stable boys all night and feeling such deep hopelessness when I would lose my precious gold to them.

I had mourned my parent's passing, but that melancholy was quickly overshadowed by my need to be reacquainted with my new wealth. I had become so preoccupied with it that my town and its tenants suffered. It wasn't long before they came for my gold. The townspeople demanded it for food and repairs. They said it was once theirs and that I owed it to them if I was not going to make sure they were provided for. With little choice, I was forced to give it up, or they would've gleefully removed my head from my shoulders.

Desperation sent me stumbling into *The Woods*, clutching a handful of gold coins I had managed to save. I threw myself at the mercy of the demon who lived there and begged him to fulfill my desires. I said I would pay any price to be able to find and keep as much gold as I possibly could forever.

I'll never forget his smile, his long tongue sweeping over his sharp teeth, and the pain that followed as we shook hands on our deal. I watched in horror as my skin began to peel back and green scales began to surface. One after another, overlapping until I was covered in them. Razor-sharp claws grew from my fingers. I remember stumbling back a step as I felt a new weight on my back and at the base of my spine. Wings and a tail sprouted from me, and as the demon cackled, I shot into the sky, illuminating it with a burst of fire from deep within my stomach.

It burned my throat and clogged my nostrils. I wasn't the most graceful flyer but I somehow found this cave. One that I've been filling with my treasures ever since. I take from the rich, the people I once was just like. I rob them of their spoils before someone else can take them. I keep them here with me, where I can protect them, guard them...*watch* them.

I've lost track of how long I've been like this. Centuries if I had to guess. Everyone who once knew the man I was is long gone, and I'm beginning to realize all these years spent alone with my treasure have turned me into more of a beast than a man.

Old memories are hazy at best. The only thing I am certain of is that I need more gold. I always need more gold; it's the only constant in my life. Without it, what would I do? I couldn't lead a normal life, not like this. I could never find a wife or make a family, the humans I come in contact with flee upon seeing me.

No one dares venture this far into *The Woods*. A few of the other creatures used to try and trade with me, but they've all gone quiet these last few years. The Kraken came by and gave me a bag of jewels. It feels like it was only yesterday, but I know that was at least a decade ago. He said something as he left them, but I can't remember it.

I've never desired anything more than gold, but it's not fulfilling me like it used to for the first time in a hundred years. A part of me, perhaps the last part of my humanity, wants to feel more. That small part demands we try and make something out of this eternal life. But what? What else can we do but get more gold and ensure it's never taken from us?

"What do you think?" I ask the coins in my hand, their smooth surface glimmering in the cave's dim light. There's a storm raging outside, and the thunder rattles their piles. I can only imagine they don't have a fondness for this type of weather.

I wait for a response like the metal will grow lips after all these years and converse with me like a companion. Alas, they remain silent.

"Is there more out there for me than this? Then my daily hunts to find more gold and jewels and keep them safe with us?" I pause. "You have always been my most trusted confidants and treasured possessions; talking to you does make me feel better."

Looking around my cave, I see all of my riches laid out. Fine silks, crowns made of the heaviest gold and brightest gems, bags of diamonds, and many, *many* gold coins. They are mine, all of them, but perhaps it wouldn't be so bad to share them?

"That wouldn't be too terrible, would it?" I ask the ten gold plates stacked on my left. "Perhaps someone out there would appreciate you all as I do. Though, where I would find such a person, I don't know. It's not as if one would just walk—"

Another clap of thunder echoes through the cave, but that isn't what has me pausing. Rising from my perch on my coins, they clink as they hit the stone floor. My claws click along the cave wall, my tail dragging gently behind me. Listening carefully, I can just make out a sound over the downpour happening outside.

Footsteps. Human footsteps.

Someone is in my cave. My scales rise as smoke puffs out of my nostrils. Who dares enter my cave uninvited? Of course, I was just considering finding a companion but one with some manners, not one who just enters my dwelling unannounced.

They could be a thief coming to take my gold from me.

That thought has me charging toward the mouth of my cave. I will make whoever stumbled into my home regret doing so. My mouth opens, fire already building in my lungs. I will roast their corpse, char their flesh until—

My flame goes out when I see it. My heart beats faster; my wings sag in pleasure as I behold it. Even in the dark cave, it glows and sparkles. It is the most beautiful gold I have ever seen. Soft as silk, the pale gold flows along the dark stone floor. It's as if thousands of stars are woven between the strands. My mouth salivates; the rain must've washed in this treasure.

This is one I will delight in keeping more than the others. This rare, golden beauty is for my eyes only.

I creep closer to my prize, extending a clawed hand toward it when I stop. This isn't gold; this is hair. How had I forgotten all about the footsteps that sent me charging up here to investigate? This is my intruder?

My eyes adjust to the dim light, and I can see her fully.

She's small, shivering in a damp cloak. A human woman with beautiful golden hair and matching eyebrows. Her skin is smooth, glowing like a polished pearl. My tail sneaks out from behind me and trails up the side of her body. Her brows furrow at the touch.

Eyes like opals blink open at me. It's like she's made from jewels, a human constructed from the finest gems. The ultimate treasure for a creature like me. I open my mouth to tell her as much, but then a small flame bursts from my mouth. The embers float in the air, and my precious human shoots upright and scrambles back, shrieking.

She can't get too far, the boulder she was sitting behind stopping her movements.

This small human shakes in front of me, her soaked cloak draped around her. Her gorgeous hair is plastered to the sides of her face. I watch her chest rise and fall and feel something happening inside my own. The more I gaze at her I realize how wrong I have been.

Was there anything more beautiful than gold? Yes, her.

She who is gold come to life. A possessiveness that I've never felt before shoots through me. My desire for her eclipses the one I've felt for any other treasure. She's the ultimate find.

The only one I will ever need.

When I was a man, I wanted a family. I wanted lovers to warm my bed. Those wants faded when I found my need for gold. Now, looking at this precious human, the desires I had wanted as a man are colliding with the ones I have as a dragon.

My golden human rises on shaking legs, glancing behind her like she has a chance of escaping me. Before she can think to move, I act. Wrapping my arm around her waist and tossing her over my shoulder. She screams again and claws at my back while she tries to wiggle away from me. Her soft breasts press into my shoulder as even more desire rushes through me.

I'll never let her go, I'll explain that to her once she calms down. She'll never want for anything, I'll protect her and care for her better than any human man can. They wouldn't know how to protect something as precious as her. She is my prize now; she belongs to me.

Forever.

3

ANWYN

A dragon...a *fucking* dragon.

I've gotten myself into some interesting situations before, but this one may be the most absurd. I will myself to remain calm as he carries me deeper into the cave. He's massive, easily over seven feet tall, made up of hard muscles and tough scales. My hands brush along their cool, rugged texture as his shoulder digs into my stomach. I watch with disdain as his tail flicks back and forth in front of my face. He snatched me with precision as if kidnapping women is common for him.

For a dragon, I suppose it is.

I had been trying to find shelter from the storm. As soon as my feet had crossed into *The Woods,* the dark clouds above had cracked open on a clap of thunder, and the rain began to fall. I was soaked in an instant, slipping and sliding in the mud of the forest floor. Searching for any start of overhang to wait out the downpour, this dry cave looked like the safest place to find shelter.

Now, I wish I would've decided to rest under a tree instead.

I let out a sigh in frustration and smack my hands against his back in a feeble effort to get him to drop me. He's no more than an animal, right? That's what I remember from the stories of dragons. He's a beast. Like any wild animal, perhaps I can startle him enough to let me go and escape. My hits to his back seem to do nothing, his measured steps never faltering. From my upside-down vantage point, I can see we are getting closer to a glowing light.

His den where he's about to char and eat me if the stories are to be believed.

Not if I have any say about it.

"Let me go!" I cry. With one last ditch effort, I wrap my hand around his massive tail and give it a tug. That makes him halt, a snarl coming from his throat. Whoops. Now, I've seemed to anger him. His hands tighten on my waist as he yanks me off his shoulder and cradles me in his arms.

"I—" Searching for something to say, I stare into his yellow gaze. His eyes are so bright they make me squint as if I was staring into the sun. His lips pull back to reveal two rows of sharp teeth. A forked tongue licks over them, making me shiver. His scales cover him completely, their green color glimmering in the low light. He exhales deeply, a puff of smoke containing a few embers dancing in front of my face.

The burnt smell makes my eyes water.

"Watch it, or you're going to burn my hair off."

I try to keep the tremble out of my voice. It's not like he can understand me, but I have to show him I'm no easy prey.

Those big yellow eyes blink at me again before he continues walking us deeper into the cave.

"Sorry," he says, the words swallowed up in a growl. My

mouth drops open. Not only have I been captured by a dragon...I've been captured by a *talking* dragon. That's an interesting development, one I can use to my advantage.

After all, I have no plans on being anything's dinner.

"You can speak?" I ask for confirmation.

"Yes." He continues walking, the light in front of us getting brighter.

"I didn't know dragons could talk. All the ones in the stories are just fire-breathing village destroyers. Too busy kidnapping princesses and holding them for ransom to make small talk." The dragon merely inclines his head as if thinking over my words. The sound of the storm outside fades with each step we take.

"I've kidnapped you."

I huff a laugh and shake my head.

"I'm far from a princess, dragon. You're not getting any money for me."

If he desires a ransom payment, I can try and barter my freedom from him with the few gold coins I traveled with. I'd hate to part with them, but it's better than being eaten.

The longer he holds me I wait for fear to take over. He could easily crush me with his strong arms or slice my neck open with one of his sharp claws. How easily he could incinerate me with one deep breath.

Yet, the more he looks at me, the more I get the sense that he wants something else. There's an emotion in his gaze that I can't name, and it unsettles me. I've relied on my ability to read people for years, but this dragon confuses me. No matter what happens, I can't let my guard drop around him. The first moment I have to escape, I must take it.

"You're far more precious than gold," he says finally.

My brows furrow at his statement. Men have flirted with me before, way before an age where it was appropriate to...

but a *dragon*? Now that's a new one. None of the stories about dragons I've ever encountered mentioned them wanting a human beyond ransoming or eating. He shifts me closer to his chest, and I gasp when I feel something hard pressing against me.

His cock is pushing softly against my side. I look up at him wide-eyed and realize what that unnamed emotion in his gaze is. Desire. He wants me. It's easy enough to surmise for what as my breathing speeds up. I could use this to my advantage as I have before. Play into his lust for me and then give him the slip.

It may prove harder to do with a dragon, but he's a male. All males think with their cocks. It won't be the first time I've flirted with one, only to take what I've needed and fled.

The glowing light ahead gets more intense, breaking me from my thoughts. The dragon carries me into his lair, where another shocked gasp leaves my lips.

Surveying my surroundings, this predicament may turn out to be quite a lucrative situation.

Gold, so much gold it hurts my eyes to look at it. Piles of sparkling coins cover the entire stone floor. There are massive chests with their lids peeled back, revealing heaps of glimmering jewels and polished gold bars. Crystals, necklaces, and even a few crowns litter the stacks. There is a pallet in front of an unlit firepit made up of a dozen overstuffed pillows and the softest-looking silks. Sconces and torches hang from the stalactite on the cave ceiling.

One bag full of treasure in here would keep me set for life. My mouth waters at the thought of the security these riches could bring me. No more odd jobs, no more running. I could buy a place of my own and live there comfortably for the rest of my days.

My plans have changed. The goal now is to escape from

the dragon with as much of this gold as I can carry before he's the wiser.

The dragon walks me over to the silk pallet and sets me down. Without this body heat, I'm aware of how soaked my clothes are and begin to shiver. The dragon's eyes narrow on my shaking form, and he turns towards the fire pit. His shoulders move as he inhales deeply, producing a burst of hot, orange flames that ignite the dry logs in the center of the pit.

It is not long before the space becomes deliciously warm, and I extend my hand toward the fire. The flames warm my fingers as the chill from the storm is melted away.

The both of us stand there for a moment, facing the flames and absorbing their warmth. My eyes close as the heat dries the hair around my face. Untying my sodden cloak, I let it pool at my feet. I hear the dragon's tail slide through a few coins littering the ground around us. His large chest rattles with each deep breath as I feel him move closer to me. Before I can open my eyes, I feel his claw slice through the leather band holding back my braided hair.

Shock at his actions renders me immobile.

My blonde tresses spill down my back as his claws shift through the strands. His touch is gentle. He works his way from the bottom of my hair toward the top of my head. His claws lightly scratch my scalp, and I have to swallow my moan. I shouldn't be enjoying this, but my hair seems to be distracting him enough to keep from eating me.

Over and over, his claws glide through my hair and brush along my scalp. My eyes feel heavy at the sensation. I can feel his large body at my back, his warm breath tickling the tops of my ears. I'm distracted by how good this sensation is I don't register just how low his claws have traveled until I feel them at the back of my gown.

With one quick cut of his claw, the lacings of my gown are severed, and the wet garment hits the floor with a soft smack. My eyes fly open as I wrap my arms around myself, naked except for my thin shift. I spin towards him as he rears back at my sudden movement.

Now I'm shocked for a new reason.

"You can't just undress me!" I don't care who this dragon is; if he can talk, then he might as well have some manners. My eyes stray lower to the simple leather breeches he wears. The outline of his hard cock is easy enough to spot. My heart pounds at the sheer size of it. If that is what he desires from me, he won't get it. Especially not after he disrobed me without permission.

Dragon males are no different from human men, it would seem, taking without asking.

"Your clothes were wet," he says simply as if that justifies it.

"That doesn't matter. You can't just undress a person without asking." I bend at the waist, pick up a silk blanket, and cover myself. His yellow eyes follow my every movement until we are staring at each other once again. He looks like he wants to say something, but then my stomach growls. The sound echoes in this deep cavern.

"You're hungry?"

I shake my head at his question; eating is the last thing I want to do despite what my body has indicated.

"I'm just tired." My traitorous stomach growls again.

The dragon gives a sharp nod and then takes a step back from me.

"I will get you food." He turns and takes another step, his tail overturning a golden goblet sending it clattering to the floor. I gasp at the blatant disregard for it. A dented cup seems to mean very little when you have this much wealth.

The dragon pauses, casting a glance at me over his shoulder.

"You are not to leave the cave."

I raise my brows. I'm not agreeing to that; as soon as he leaves to hunt, I'm gathering as much as I can carry and bolting out of here. I could fill the goblet he had just knocked over with enough diamonds to buy a hundred dresses to replace the one he just destroyed.

The dragon turns back to me and stomps closer. His body is mere inches from mine, and I have to crane my neck up to make eye contact with him. His nostrils flare as he breathes in my scent. His fork tongue slips out to lick over his scaled lips.

"What is your name, precious one?" he asks.

"Anwyn," I say. There's no need to waste a good alias on a dragon. His tongue licks over his lips again, savoring what I just said. He inhales deeply once more, his scales flexing with the movement, before shaking himself slightly.

"I'm sorry, my precious Anwyn, but I can't risk it. I must keep my treasure safe."

Before I can ask what he's doing, he moves, grabbing me by the waist and dragging me over to a stalagmite on the cave floor. I thrash in his grip, but he holds firm. My eyes widen in horror as I see the golden shackle already mounted into the stone. Grabbing my wrists, he chains them each in a golden shackle.

They are not tight enough to hurt, but there is no way to break free unless I plan to shatter my hand. I pull against the restraints, the cold metal pressing into my skin. The dragon takes a few steps back from me, his eyes remorseful.

"What are you doing? Let me go!" I screech, trying in vain to break free. The shackles clank against the rock. With one last mighty pull, I sink to my knees as my bound wrists hang in front of me.

The dragon opens his mouth but quickly shuts it. He's gone from my kidnapper to my jailer. He may desire me, but I am no more than a trinket like the ones that litter this cave. I will break free of these chains and make him regret ever capturing me.

With that resolve in mind, I watch silently as massive wings peel and snap from the skin of his back. They expand behind him, the green scales glittering in the firelight. Comprised completely of thick muscles with sharp claws decorating the bottoms, they are as deadly as they are magnificent.

The dragon says nothing more as he launches into the air. His wings thunder with each powerful flap, causing the air to swirl around me and tangle my hair. His clawed feet leave the stone floor as he turns and flies swiftly toward the mouth of the cave. Leaving a trail of rattling gold coins in his wake.

4

LASSAR

Anwyn.

It's fitting that a woman as lovely as my precious Anwyn would have the most perfect name ever crafted. *Gods*, she is beautiful. Each moment I spent in her company, she only became more beautiful.

And when she spoke? I could barely hold back from claiming her right then and there. She wouldn't have liked that, my precious one. Undressing her had been a mistake. I had only desired to help relieve her of her wet clothes, but she was right. I shouldn't have done it without her permission. I've been in this beastly form for so long that I hardly have any memories of how you are supposed to court a woman as perfect as Anwyn.

She told me she is no princess, and that is true. Anwyn is more than just a title. More than any station or jewel or fine cloth. There is a fire roaring in her opal eyes, one that matches my own. I feel it simmering under the surface.

When I brought her down to my lair, I felt many emotions from her. Apprehension, which is reasonable. Then anger when I cut her dress, followed by rage when I chained her to the floor. I meant what I said to her; I can't risk my treasure. She is the best treasure I have ever found and I will not allow her to sneak off while I gather food.

The thought of providing a meal to her makes my mouth water and my cock harden. To be able to provide for my precious one is a treat I've never experienced. My cock has been hard for her since I first saw her behind that boulder. It only got more persistent the longer I carried her in my arms. Her skin is as smooth and pale. It begs for my touch, my tongue.

I shiver at the thought of tasting her bare skin. Of tracing those delicate curves hidden by her shift. I'd sever the wings from my back for just one lick of her little pussy. To spread her out before me and feast on her warm, wet flesh. It would fill me with more satisfaction than a hundred trunks filled with gold.

Damp leaves snag in my scales, and I realize I've dropped into the tree line. Thoughts of Anwyn have made me lose focus on my task at hand. Bringing her food so that she is comfortable and will see me as someone who can take care of her as she needs. She'll never want for anything in my care.

I'll make sure of it.

I hit the edge of *The Woods* with a silent thud. The storm is still raging. Freezing rain covers me. I puff a small flame in between my hands to warm them. It was a miracle my treasure found her way to my cave. I can't even think of what would've become of her had she tried to push through this storm.

In front of me is a small village. A long time ago, when I was still more human, I would barter with a few of the townsfolk. Over the years, I've slipped a few trinkets from the more wealthy inhabitants. One of whose home sits just in front of me. It is about five times larger than any of the ones around it. A warm orange glow can be seen through the windows while its chimney sends smoke into the storming sky.

The wealthiest member of the town has always lived in this house. It's been a while since I pilfered through a human's home, but my Anwyn deserves the finest things. This house will surely have what I need, and then I can return to my precious one.

Overhead, the storm rages on. The sheets of rain conceal me in the dark as I fly to the top of the house. Landing silently on the sod roof, I peel back enough of the grass and soil to peer inside. My wings keep my peephole free of any rain so I don't risk exposure by the home's inhabitants.

The inside of the house is warm. Everything is cast in a golden glow by the roaring fireplace. Fine china and silver goblets decorate an ornately carved wooden table with matching wooden chairs. There are fine paintings and tapestries that line the walls that would normally snag my attention first. However, I can't help but compare their brilliance to Anwyn's.

Now that I have glimpsed the rarest jewel, all other treasures are as unremarkable as tin by comparison.

What does capture my attention is the wide assortment of bottled wines decorating the far wall. Reds, whites, sparkling...I wonder what kind is Anwyn's favorite? I shall have to get her a variety and see.

The smell of roasting meats wafts toward me, making my mouth water. The closest I've come to cooking in years was charing the animals I killed with some of my flames. However, this roasted chicken looks beautifully prepared. Garnished with whipped potatoes and green beans, the

hardy meal should provide my Anwyn with enough suste-
nance for all the things I want to do with her.

My cock hardens even further as I break from those
thoughts. I must stay focused on getting her food and less
on getting her naked even if it is the most difficult thing I
have ever done.

The home below me is quiet. I watch as a servant in
simple wool clothes makes a plate from the roast and sides
dishes cooking over the fire. With shaking hands, he walks
the plate back over to the table and sets it down at a place
setting. The goblet of wine sitting there is filled with dark
red wine.

It isn't long until the hinges of the old wooden door
creak open. A new scent enters the home, and I peer
through the sod roof to inspect who's just arrived. The man
is wealthy, which is evident from his fine clothing, but they
are almost too gaudy. Unlike the fine attire I was used to as a
Lord, his garments are not comprised of good quality mate-
rials but rather of those that sparkle the most.

His thinning dark hair is damp from the rain. The
wooden table rattles as he sits down and gulps down the
wine, wiping his mouth with the back of his wrinkled hand.
Even as a dragon, I balk at his overwhelming lack of
manners.

"That will be all tonight, Jonathan. See to it that you get
some rest, for I will need you back here before first light." A
cruel smile tugs at the lips around his goblet. "I am to wed at
dawn."

A pang of reget hits me. My humanity may have less-
ened over the years, but for Anwyn, I feel some of it slowly
creeping back. I want to be better for her, someone worthy
of her. Would she be okay with me stealing from a man

before his wedding night? My precious one has a kind heart, I can tell.

I will just take what's necessary for her and find more legitimate ways to secure the supplies she needs in the future.

The old servant snaps up straight.

"Married?" Jonathan chokes. "I mean—who is the lucky bride, Mr. Wicksome?"

"The girl who's been living with Mrs. Hitherbend." Mr. Wicksome stabs the roast chicken and takes a meaty bite, the grease coating his lips. "Anwyn, she calls herself."

My chest tightens, and the fire in my throat gathers, demanding I release it on this foul creature who covets my precious one.

"Anwyn? But she is but a girl—"

"She is young and healthy. And I think I will very much enjoy bedding her until she is with child." Mr. Wicksome's tongue licks over his teeth. "Unlike my former wretch of a wife, I have no doubt Anwyn will give me the heirs I need."

"Very good, sir," the servant mutters, slipping on his coat. "I shall be off then."

I watch Mr. Wicksome gulp down more wine as a rage I have never known spreads through my body. It tickles every scale and makes the sod roof shred in my claws. My wings draw back tight as my vision is consumed in red.

The last time I was this angry was just after I had been cursed. The rage then didn't burn as acutely as this.

Mr. Wicksome pours more wine into his goblet, laughing to himself.

This is why my Anwyn ventured into the storm. I should be grateful; his clearly unwanted proposal of marriage sent her right to me. However, I find myself anything but. This man, this *vermin*, covets my treasure. He seeks to steal her from me and keep her for his own. He'll never touch her; no one ever will. She is mine.

Mine to keep, mine to possess, mine to protect.

He thinks to bed her? To breed her? He is the reason she was almost lost to the storm tonight. And for that, as the protector of my precious one, he must pay with his life, of course. Endangering my Anwyn deserves the most severe punishment.

No longer caring about keeping my presence a secret, I rip the sod roof off with my claws and swoop down. Mr. Wicksome gags on his bite of chicken as I yank him from the table and pin him against a wooden beam. His beady eyes grow wide, my hand collaring his neck digs in, and my claws make his blood flow down his neck in slow rivulets.

A puff of dark smoke is expelled from my mouth, the taste burning my tongue. With his limited air, Mr. Wicksome coughs and splutters. Water splatters at my feet. I half believe it to be more rain coming in from the ruined roof until the scent of urine invades my nose.

This weakling of a man sought out my treasure? He was never a match for her. In her name, I will eradicate this threat.

"You sought out my treasure?" I growl into his reddening face.

"I—you...I—" he chokes.

"You sought to take my Anwyn from me? You're the reason I almost lost her in the storm?"

"Your Anwyn—"

"Don't!" I roar. "Don't you ever say her name, mortal. Don't you ever think about her again."

"I won't—I swear it!" he vows. I feel my grip lessen as he sucks down more air. His promise should cool some of my anger, but it doesn't. If anything, I feel angrier. I hear his crude words about my precious Anwyn float back to me. He was going to marry her and breed her, clearly without her consent.

The more I stare at this pathetic excuse for a man, the more my beast roars at me to take action. To stop this threat against Anwyn now. And permanently. This human is a pig.

Everyone knows the best type of pig is a roasted one.

"I don't think I'm going to give you the chance to."

Without warning, I breathe in, allowing the fire in my stomach to rage and roar. With one mighty exhale, my flames shoot forward, warming the scales on my nose. Mr. Wicksome screams as his body is charred. The hands he thought to touch my Anwyn with, the mouth he thought to kiss her with are reduced to ash in a matter of moments. His smoking corpse lies at my feet.

I was wrong. My humanity is still lost when it comes to Anwyn. The only difference is I want to be that creature. The one that sends fears into the hearts of all who behold it so that she may stay safe in my company.

I have no remorse as I find a discarded satchel and stuff it full of wine, meats, and cheeses. As I load the still-warm dinner into the bag and cast one last look at the man who I killed for it.

I am happy to have eradicated this threat to my precious one. Bending at my knees, I fan my wings and take to the sky. It's time to return to her, my prize. With my supplies in hand, it's now time for me to show her I'm the only one who can keep her safe and truly provide for her.

Now, I must show her why she should stay with me forever.

5

ANWYN

The thunder of large wings echoing through the cave has me looking up.

With a frustrated sigh, I throw the golden coin I was using to unscrew the shackles from the floor. I've been trying to free myself for the better part of an hour but was unsuccessful. Now my jailer has returned, and my chance of escaping just became nonexistent. Sitting with my back against the stalagmite, I hear his wings getting closer.

The cool stone sinks into my skin, damp with sweat from my escape attempt.

Foolish. Instead of wasting time on my restraints, I should've tried to locate some sort of weapon. Then waited for him to unlock me and, no doubt, feast on my flesh and then take that opportunity to attack. I may not have killed him, but at least wounded him enough to flee. Now through narrowed eyes, I watch his massive form lower to the ground with apprehension.

His glowing gaze locks on me, his leather pants dripping water onto the stone floor. From around his massive chest, he loops a worn leather satchel over his head and sets it down gently in front of the pallet by the fire. The old bag looks like it's about to burst with whatever is contained inside. My stomach growls as he takes out the contents.

The bag rattles as he makes a place setting of a silver plate and matching goblet. Next, he brings forth a still steaming roasted chicken, followed by a bowl of potatoes and green beans. There is an assortment of bread rolls, cheese, and ten different bottles of wine. My mouth is surely watering by the time he steps back.

His yellow eyes return to me as if seeking my approval. My stomach clenches, and for the moment, I don't care what his motives are for this food. I would be a fool to refuse a hearty meal like this one. At the very least, it will give me enough strength should the opportunity to escape arise.

The dragon is still looking at me expectantly, and I raise my shackled wrist, letting the metal click together. He moves quickly, using a dark claw to unlock the clasp. I rub my wrists and watch remorse swim in his eyes. He's the one who chained me up so I wouldn't rob him. Of course, that's exactly what I intend to do.

Silently, I follow him to the pallet on the floor. He watches me again, his massive chest rising and falling as I sink to the floor, careful to avoid his tail that lies at my feet. I pick up the fork left out for me and take a bite of the potatoes. Their rich, creamy texture melts on my tongue. I have to swallow down a moan as I go for another bite.

"How is the food?" the dragon asks, his massive wings folding into his back.

I toss my hair over my shoulder and shrug.

"The potatoes are cold."

His head snaps back, and I think I've angered him. I don't know what possessed me to say it. Perhaps it is my frustration with the situation. If he wanted a nice dinner companion, the first step would be not kidnapping and chaining them to his floor.

His massive shoulders sag, and he snatches my plate from me.

Oh great, now I've done it. I watch as he walks over to the roaring fire, his clawed feet clicking along the stone. The fire has burned down, but he quickly adds more logs until it is roaring once more. My eyes begin to water, knowing I'm about to watch him burn the food he brought me. Mouthing off to a dragon was going to have consequences, and now I'm going to spend what could be my last night in this world starving.

I should've just eaten the cold potatoes.

The dragon spends a few minutes over by the fire. With each one that passes, I grow more and more curious when I don't hear the sizzle of the food being dumped out on them. After another moment, he returns the plate of food steaming in his hands. He sets it down in front of me.

"Be careful, my Anwyn, the plate will be hot. I do not wish for you to burn your precious skin." *So he can do it himself later*, I think, but I only nod my head. Perhaps, I am being too harsh on this dragon. After all, none of the stories mentioned them braving a storm to ensure their victims were fed. Of course, he could have his own motives for this, but the look of absolute pleasure on his face as I eat my meal tells me there's something else going on here.

Still, I'm just grateful to have a meal.

Once I have polished off most of the food, he uncorks a bottle of red wine with a claw and fills my goblet. I take a small sip. It is just as delicious as well. The meal and now the wine has caused my body to become more relaxed. The dragon next to me takes another deep inhale through his nose, his tail grazing the bottom of my feet and the sides of my legs ever so often.

"Do you like the wine?" he asks. Reaching over, I pluck the bottle up, wondering if I smashed it, would a jagged piece of the glass be enough to penetrate his scales? Surely not, but I file that information away for later.

The bottle almost slips from my hand as I see the seal stamped onto the front of the bottle. The Wicksome seal. My head jerks up as I look the dragon in the eyes, my mouth parting.

"Where...where did you get this wine?" I gesture down to my lap, where my plate sits. "This food?"

My heart pounds and blood roars in my ears. The dragon sits up straighter, a fierce look on his face.

"From the human man called Wicksome. The one who wished to marry you," he growls out. His yellow eyes blaze hot, turning into molten gold. A puff of smoke exits his nostrils, warning of the fire inside him.

"Did you tell him you had me?" I ask. If Mr. Wicksome comes here, I'll be trading one jailer for another. At least with this dragon, my suffering will be short. Mr. Wicksome intends to make me suffer for the rest of my life. I can't afford to be found by him, I won't be. The broken glass may not be enough to puncture this dragon's scales, but it will be sharp enough to slice a human throat.

The dragon shakes his head, his tail whipping behind him.

"I've taken care of him. I'd never endanger my most precious possession."

"He'd want your gold to be sure," I say, gesturing around me. "But I'm worried he'd follow you here and take me back to the village. I have no desire to marry a man like that."

Any man, really.

The dragon shakes his head again.

"He will never come after you, my Anwyn. I left his burning corpse in his dining room before I returned to you."

My mouth drops open as my heart thunders in my chest.

"You killed him?" I ask incredulously. "Why? To steal all of this?"

His golden eyes are tender on my face. He reaches out a clawed hand, and I will myself to remain still as he tucks a stay piece of hair behind my ear. Goosebumps break out along my skin as his claw tickles the shell of my ear.

"To make you safe. That man scared you so much with his threats of marriage you set off into a storm that could've killed you. I would not allow such a man as that to live." The dragon takes my plate and rises. "I will get you more food, my Anwyn."

I'm at a loss for words as I watch him at the fire. The flames illuminate his muscular back in greens and yellows. As he prepares more food for me, I let my mind fully absorb what he's just told me.

Mr. Wicksome is...*dead*. Burnt to a crisp. I'm free from that danger, because of the dragon in front of me.

Something unnamed worms its way into my chest. *To make you safe. That man scared you so much...I would not allow such a man as that to live.* The words the dragon said float back to me. For the first time in a long time, I feel...protected.

Not since before my parents both perished have I felt this way. That someone was looking out for me, taking care of me, solving my problems for me. It's always just been me, fending for myself. However, this dragon solved a major problem for me. Albeit with a more permanent solution but he did it for me.

Because Mr. Wicksome scared me.

When another plate of steaming food is set down in front of me, I look up at him. Have I been too swift to judge him? Are his true motives as nefarious as I believe? If he just wanted to eat me, surely he wouldn't have gone to all the trouble of getting me food.

I allow myself to relax for the first time in a long time. There is no danger present here, and it's clear he's not going to try and eat me. Yet, that is.

"Thank you," I say softly, not knowing if I'm giving him thanks for the food or for slaying Mr. Wicksome. He nods, his scaled lips twisting, making me believe he's trying to smile. That hardening bulge in his leather trousers is ever-present. While it scared me before, I now see it as something else entirely. An assurance that this dragon's lust for me, as ludicrous as that sounds, may just outweigh his desire to eat me.

At the very least, I can play into it and try and convince him to release me. My tactics have been all wrong. Brute force and surprise attacks won't aid me. As nonsensical as it sounds, it's the option I've been presented with: I'm going to flirt with a dragon.

Relaxing my shoulders, I tuck some more hair behind my ear and reach for the plate. Taking another bite, I moan softly, noting his changing posture. I chuckle quietly and look up at him, where he looms above me through my lashes.

"What is your name? I assume you have one. After all you've done for me, I find it rude to keep referring to you as *dragon*."

"Lassar," he says, coming down to sit beside me. I lean back, letting the silk blanket I'm still wearing drop off my shoulder. His gaze licks over the slope of my shoulder as my stomach flutters. This feels different than when I've flirted with men in the past. It was about stroking their ego, making them feel powerful. But the longer I say under Lassar's golden stare, I find myself becoming the powerful one.

It seems this dragon would be content to just stare at me until the end of time.

"Interesting name, for a dragon, I mean." I furrow my brows. "Though, I don't recall the dragons in the stories ever having any names. Beyond *destruction-bringer*, of course."

Lassar nods his head, his lips pulling into what I can now confidently say is his version of a smile.

"I was not always a dragon."

"Oh?" I ask.

"I was a man once. A lord. From a kingdom on the other side of *The Woods,* a long time ago." There's a sadness in his honey eyes, and my hand moves to touch him, to comfort him. I stop myself before I do, shocked by my body's response. This is a part I'm playing, I don't care about this man-turned-dragon at all.

Right?

"How did you become like this?" I ask. Lassar is silent for a moment, and I think he isn't going to answer. His claws scrape along the floor, picking up a gold coin. The metal shimmers in the dim light, and Lassar shakes his head.

"I made a bargain with the demon who lives here. I came to him a greedy mortal; my only care in the world was gold. Having it, keeping it, hoarding it, and then finding more. It consumed me day and night. I came to him asking if there was a way for me to have endless amounts of gold." He closes his fist around the coin, scales flexing over his knuckles. "The demon told me there was a way to have more gold than any man in this land. In my desirous state, I took the deal, and it wasn't until a few moments later when my bones began to snap, and scales grew through my skin, I realized that I had made a terrible mistake."

"Lassar, I—" But what can I even say? His anguish is clear. A greedy man who has amassed such wealth all for it to mean nothing ultimately. No one to share it with, no companions. A lonely, sparkling life. The demon of *The Woods* is just as foul as the rumors about him suggest.

More than anything, though, I understand Lassar a bit more. More gold would certainly fix my problems. After all these years of running, I could buy my own home and be safe and alone. As I look around this beautiful cave, filled with treasures only kings would dream of, I wonder if my own life isn't heading in the same path as Lassar's.

"I do not wish to burden you, my Anwyn, with such a sad tale." He reaches out slowly and skims a claw down the side of my cheek. "The curse is not all bad; it's the reason I have you now."

I laugh and shake my head.

"That's true, it's odd that my path would cross with a dragon before a rich lord, but here we are."

"And I am grateful for it. A rich lord wouldn't have appreciated you as he should," he says, and I duck my head. The raw emotion in his eyes makes me look away. My hand rubs along my wrist, no marks are left, but they still feel sore. Lassar makes a sound in his throat. "I'm sorry for shackling you. I just couldn't risk it, Anwyn, especially not now."

I look up and meet his eyes.

"I understand, Lassar. You gave up your humanity for this gold. It's reasonable that you would want to protect it at all costs."

His mouth opens slightly, and he leans forward. My spine straightens as his face comes closer to mine. For a moment, I think he may kiss me. Instead of being scared or disgusted, I find myself intrigued by the possibility of what those scaled lips would feel like against my own.

An absurd thought.

I don't find out what his lips are like, but the breath is stolen from me all the same when he speaks these next words against my lips. All of them are far more precious than jewels could ever be.

"My gold isn't the treasure I was worried about keeping safe." My heart pounds in my chest as his eyes glow brighter in the dark cave. My thighs squeeze together as his warm breath bathes my lips.

"It was you."

6

LASSAR

Anwyn is not asleep, though she pretends to be.

I've stuffed enough pillows and silk blankets under her to make sure the hard floor doesn't come in contact with her delicate skin. The fire burns next to her, the flames licking over her small body assure me that she is warm enough. However, I can tell she's awake. Her form is too stiff under the silk blanket, her breathing too uneven.

Still, I stay vigilant as I watch over her from my perch in the corner.

Now that I have my precious Anwyn, I must always stay on guard so she can rest peacefully, knowing I'm watching over her. My Anwyn is so lovely. Albeit a bit quiet. After I had confessed to her being my treasure and not this frivolous gold around me, she had polished off her wine and gone silent. Only spoke to tell me she was ready for bed, and I got to work making her pallet on the floor.

From the moment she settled into the mess of blankets and pillows, I have watched over her.

Anwyn gives a sigh and rolls onto her back before

rolling onto her side to face me. The firelight makes her glow like a goddess, and I lean forward. Is she too cold? Too hot? Is she hungry again? Her cheeks are too hollow for my liking.

It's late, but if I set off now, I could—

"I can't sleep with you watching me like that," she says, her soft voice echoing around us. I gesture toward the mouth of the cave with my claws.

"You are my most precious possession, Anwyn. If I lower my guard, someone may come and try and take you from me." I cross my arms over my chest and give her a sharp nod. "I will not fail you. I will keep watch over you while you sleep."

Anwyn wrinkles her small nose.

"No one is coming after me now that you've roasted Wicksome."

"Is there no one else looking for you? A family?"

Anwyn shakes her head, her golden hair moving about her shoulders. A loneliness swims in her eyes, one that I am all too familiar with. We are both lonely creatures. There may be more similarities between me and my precious one than I thought.

Anwyn lets out another sigh and sits up, the blanket wrapped around her revealing her shoulders. My mouth waters at the sight of her. Tucking some loose hair behind her ears, she squares her shoulders at me.

"Look, you need to stop staring at me." She takes another breath as if summoning her strength. Her eyes are wary as they bore into mine, and I brace myself for what she is about to say next. "I'll need to be well rested so I can set off in the morning."

My flames roar in my stomach and climb up my throat, begging me to expel them. She wants to leave. My precious

Anwyn wants to leave me. The way she's holding herself, I can tell she's waiting for me to explode, to forbid her from going. I suppose I could do that, but I want her willing. I would never imprison my lovely Anwyn; only for her own safety did I keep her.

I am a monster, to be sure, but I will be a monster *for* her, never towards her.

The flames inside me fizzle, and my shoulders drop. I did not provide my Anwyn with enough. Even though I tried my best to show her I was the only one who could keep her safe, it's clear it was not enough, and she has decided to set out on her own. I've failed, I've lost my chance to keep her forever.

Now that I know she is alive, I'll watch over her from the shadows for eternity. Protecting her in the best way that I can until she thinks to give me another chance. And if she does not, watching over her will give me more pleasure than a million gold coins.

I give a sharp nod, the only response I can muster towards her statement that will not show the pain her choice has caused me. The acute disappointment I feel towards myself.

Anwyn's opal eyes glow with surprise, but she says nothing, just lies back down on her mountain of pillows. The moments tick on as I watch her beautiful face look up at the ceiling of the cave. Her head turns toward me again.

"You're still staring."

"I can't risk it. I must keep watch over you." This I will hold firm on. I will never let harm come to her. Anwyn gives another sigh and then pats the space beside her. My brows lower at the action.

"If you're so worried about someone coming and

stealing me, then you can lay right next to me. I can't sleep feeling your eyes on me like that."

My heart pounds in my chest. Lay beside her? Feel the warmth of her body? My mouth begins to water in earnest. My precious Anwyn has given me the ultimate gift. To spend this last night in my lair pressed close together.

I try not to trip over my own tail in my haste to make my way over to her pallet.

Anwyn shuffles over and turns onto her side, facing away from me. Her sweet scent invades my senses; the warmth of her body soaks into my scales. My body screams at me to touch her, trace her curves with my claws, and taste her skin with my tongue. I burn with the need to grab her and hold her to me, to show her the pleasure I and I alone can give her.

That's when it hits me.

I haven't shown her the extent of my devotion, the pleasure I wish to bring her. Sure, I've gotten her food and made her warm, but I haven't shown her the euphoria I can bring her with my mouth and my cock. Would she like me to? It may be the only way to keep her with me. If I give her a taste of the pleasure that could be hers for eternity if she chose to remain at my side.

It's worth the risk.

Her body shifts next to mine. I turn to face her, leaving only a few inches of space between us. With another sigh, she tries to relax her body. The movement causes her to slide the reaming distance towards me. The supple mounds of her ass press into my cock. Anwyn lets out a small gasp as her body goes still.

With a few small manipulations from my tail, I slowly drag the silk blanket covering her down her body. The fire and my body will keep her warm enough. It's not long until the smooth skin of her arm is revealed. My tongue tries to slide out of my mouth to lick it, but I hold back. Instead, I carefully run my claw from her shoulder to her wrist. Her precious flesh breaks out in goosebumps, and she lets out a moan. My cock is so hard that I fear it may shatter before I've gotten the chance to pleasure her with it.

I trace up the side of her exposed arm one more time before she twists to look at me. Her opal eyes are heavy-lidded.

"What are you doing?" she asks.

"Making sure my precious Anwyn is relaxed."

"I—" Anwyn lets out another moan. This is my opportunity to show her what I can provide her, I will not waste it. She is not pushing me away, and that strengthens my resolve.

"Will you let me help you sleep, my Anwyn?" I whisper near her ear. She shivers and turns so that our eyes meet. There is so much swirling in her opal irises, different emotion warring there. I wait for her answer, my heart continuing to pound. With another deep breath, she closes her eyes and gives me one small nod.

I let out a growl and waste no time servicing my precious one.

Wrapping my arm around her waist, I pull her back tight against my front. She releases another moan as my hard cock presses more firmly against her. Leaning my head down, I run my nose along her neck, reveling in the feel of her soft skin against my hard scales. Her scent consumes me, sweet like the ripest fruits, I want to swallow and drink it down. To bathe in her essence for the rest of my days. My forked tongue slips from my mouth and follows the path my nose just made up her throat.

Her scent deepens as I take my time on the delicate skin

of her neck. Licking and biting and sucking until a pink mark is left behind. The sight of me marking her has my blood pumping even faster, the fire inside of me growing even hotter. Anwyn's plump lips puff open, and my mouth seeks to claim them, but not yet. I need to savor her; if I taste her now, I won't be able to control myself.

My clawed hand skims over her stomach and up her chest. I feel her pounding heart as my fingers slip just inside the top of her shift. I wait for a moment to see if she protests, but when she continues breathing heavily, her eyes glassy with lust, I continue. Slowly, I slip beneath the neckline of her shift and trail along the soft swells of her breasts.

I grasp one in my hand. Her breasts are perfect, small, and round. I gently knead one while she writhes and moans, stopping only to thumb her hard nipple. I had lovers as a human, but none of them made me feel like how Anwyn does. To allow me to do this to her in this monstrous form? She truly is a gift I don't deserve, and I will do everything to make sure she doesn't regret this.

My tail follows my hand's lead. Gently it creeps up the hem of her shift; it traces up the side of her calf, over the soft skin of her knee and thigh. Her skin is deliciously warm. Back and forth, it skims over her inner thighs, inching closer to that sweet spot between her legs. Already her thighs have grown damp for me.

Anwyn looks back at me, her opal eyes wide and wild.

"N—no one has ever touched me there," she says breathlessly. My snarl is ripped from my lips. My Anwyn has saved herself for me. Even if she didn't know she was, I'm the one who will win the honor of being able to claim her.

My tail trails up higher and traces her wet slit with its blunt end. Her little cunt is soaking wet and hot. Anwyn thrashes next to me, her moan singing in my ears. I rub her over and over again, my tail becoming slick with her arousal. Her chest rises and falls, my claws lightly digging into the skin of her breast.

"Are you going to let me make you come, my precious Anwyn?"

Again, my tail presses more firmly against her clit. Her back arches, and her small hands grasp my forearm around her waist. Her eyes are wild as they look at me, and she nods furiously. With a growl, I double the efforts of my tail. Rubbing her, gliding through her wet flesh, pressing gently into her entrance. Over and over again until her whole body is trembling.

"Please, Lassar. Please kiss me," she moans, leaning her head back and bringing her lips close to mine.

Who am I to deny my precious one?

My mouth comes down on hers, and my head spins. Her lips are full and soft as they gently press against mine. She holds on to my arm tighter as she sighs, my tail never ceasing its movements between her legs. My other comes up to cradle her head, my scales snagging in the long tresses of her hair. Anwyn gives a surprised gasp as my tail nudges her entrance again.

I take that small opportunity to taste her fully.

My tongue licks over the seam of her lips as they open slightly. Rolling her gently onto her back, I devour my sweet Anwyn. Her body is small beneath my own frame, reminding me to be gentle with my precious one. Her mouth opens for me, and I sweep my tongue inside. Hers is tentative as it tangles with my own, her sweet taste amplified.

Her legs fall on either side of me as I settle between them. The delicious heat from her pussy warms my cock through my pants. I grind against her, swallowing down each moan she gives me. Anwyn's small hands glide up my back, sinking into the muscles and scales there.

"Lassar," she slurs, "please, I need more."

"Then I'll give you more, Anwyn." My tongue licks up the side of her neck, its forked end tickling her ear. "I'm the only one who will satisfy this pussy. This is what you need from me, isn't it? To take care of the ache between your thighs."

"Yes!" she cries, her pupils blown wide with pleasure.

My hips drop down as I grind against her mercilessly. Her arousal soaks through my pants as I dry-fuck her over and over again. Soon she'll be wrapped around my cock, where I can spill my seed inside her. Marking her as mine from the inside out.

I return to her pink lips for a moment before my hands tangle in the neckline of her shift. With one tug, her breasts are freed, and I go to claim nipple with my mouth. I pull my hips back slightly and let my tail press firmly down on her clit. Her legs tremble as they lock around my hips. I continue biting and sucking her breasts. A lock of golden hair sticks to her sweaty forehead.

"Lassar, I'm going to—" Anwyn lets out a scream that echoes in the cave around us. Moisture rushes from her pussy, and my tail is there to gather as much of it as it can. Her pussy clamps gently around the tip of it while she rides out her orgasms. I look down at her breasts, covered in my marks, and my chest glows with pride.

She is mine. She was always mine.

Her legs drop from around my waist, her eyes are wild, and a delicate sheen of sweat coats her body. I stare into her brown eyes as I bring my tail to my lips and lick her come off of it. Sweeter than any wine. More color rises to her cheeks, and she tries to duck her head. Leaning down, I kiss her again, sharing her taste with her.

"Beautiful, my Anwyn. You taste like the sweetest fruit." I brush some blonde hair off of her brow. "Never hide from me, not after your little pussy just came all over my tail."

Her face warms even more.

"Lassar, that was...there are no words for it."

Anwyn lays back down on the pallet, and I watch a yawn sneak up on her. Falling down beside her, I gather her to my chest, her ass once again resting against my hard cock. It begs me to show her the pleasure I can give her with it, but not tonight. My Anwyn is tired.

"Sleep, my precious Anwyn. The sun will rise before long."

She nods, her hair tickling the underside of my chin. With her warm body in my arms and the taste of her arousal on my tongue, life seems perfect for the first time since I've been cursed to live in this infernal form. That's all thanks to the treasure who is snoring softly in my arms.

7

ANWYN

ithout opening my eyes, I can tell I'm alone. The cave is eerily quiet, with only the sporadic pops and cracks coming from the fire to break up the silence. Stretching my arms above my head, I let out a deep sigh, happy to be on my own this morning so that I'm able to reflect on the absurdity of last night.

I still feel his claws on me. Pulling down the top of my shift, I can see the faint impressions of his claws on my breasts. I've never let any man touch me like that; a few have stolen kisses in the past, but nothing like what Lassar did. He devastated my mouth with his own. His kiss was filled with so much reverence. Thinking about them, I feel my pussy growing wet again.

Watching him lick my come from his tail had almost made me climax again.

Which is ridiculous, given that he is a dragon. A dragon who kidnapped me, if nothing else. It makes little difference if he was once a man. Doesn't it? I honestly don't know. All I do know is that when I told him my plan was to leave this morning, he didn't say I had to stay.

He didn't say anything on the subject if I recall correctly; my mind still racing with the memory of what we did on the silk sheets. Perhaps it is the oddity of the whole situation, but I don't regret what happened. He had made me warm, fed me, and provided me with a mind-altering orgasm. There is a part of me, a small ridiculous part, that wants to stay here longer. Which, again, is absurd. What type of future would I have here?

A good one, a voice whispers in my head, but I ignore it.

I do plan on leaving. Now that he's gone and I have been left unshackled, I need to get a move on. Enjoying that last bit of warmth from the fire, I rise, covering myself in another silk sheet. I should ask Lassar if I can borrow this for my journey. And a few coins; it's not like he can't spare them.

My plan to slip away quietly is quickly thwarted when I hear a commotion at the front of the cave. It's only a few moments until Lassar's massive wings swoop down in the middle of the lair. His muscled back flexes as he collapses his wings. The torches have been lit, and they illuminate his emerald scales. They sparkle in the light. My cheeks heat as I remember how those scales felt on the delicate skin of my thighs.

His eyes meet mine, their gold color glowing with a hundred emotions that I have to duck my head. Again, this whole situation is ridiculous. Why am I being shy around a dragon? A dragon who protected me and killed Mr. Wicksome for scaring me. Who went out into a storm to make sure I had something to eat.

His claws click along the stone floor, his tail rattling through scattered gold coins and goblets. I keep my head down until I see him set two large leather bags at my feet.

They are covered in raindrops; if I listen closely, I can still hear the storm raging overhead.

I suppress a groan. Travel will be miserable. That is if I am still permitted to go...

As if he heard my thoughts, Lassar takes a step back and clears his throat.

"These looked like your size."

I look up at him with a brow raised, and he gestures toward the bags. Curious, I drop to my knees and begin unloading their contents. My hands tremble as I realize what he's brought me. Gowns, wool ones, and simple cotton ones in a myriad of colors. A few pairs of shoes ranging from dancing slippers to thick leather boots that will aid me today as I travel through the mud.

A loud clap of thunder echoes through the cave. My hands grip one of the wool gowns. It's so warm in this cave. The thought of traipsing through icy rain has me reconsidering leaving. Would it be so bad to stay? A least for a little while longer?

Again, as if he can read my thoughts, Lassar takes a step towards me.

"Would you like breakfast before you head out? I want to make sure you're fed, my Anwyn. You will need your strength navigating *The Woods*."

"That would be wonderful, Lassar. Thank you." Rising, I slip the new wool gown over my shift. It fits me perfectly. Smoothing my hands down the gray fabric, I look up to see Lassar back at the fire. A pan is heating over the open flame as he cracks a few eggs into it.

"Where did you get all of these things?" I ask. While I am happy to be in possession of these fine items, whoever their original owner is will need them come winter. It's not as if I haven't stolen before, but for some reason, the thought makes me regretful. Ashamed even, and I don't know why.

"I scared a human trader enough cutting through *The Woods* to take my coin in exchange for giving me what he was meant to be delivering to a nobleman's daughter." Lassar looks over at me, his scaled lips tipping into a smile. "Of course, after I assured him I was not going to eat him."

"I'm sure that was his first thought."

"Is that what your first thought of me was? That I was going to eat you," Lassar asks.

"Well—" I start, cringing at his question.

"You know I have no desire to devour any part of you." His tongue licks over his lips. "Except your pretty little cunt."

My face flames as I look away. I don't know what to say to that. I thought I'd be able to sneak away this morning before talk of last night came up but clearly, that is not the case. Lassar continues to cook in silence; the sizzling of bacon soon fills the lair with a wonderful smell. My stomach growls.

Over on my left, I notice a small wooden side table with two ornate chairs. Walking over to them, I sit down in one of the seats, my knees feeling weak after our conversation. This whole encounter has thrown me off kilter.

Lassar walks over to me and sets a steaming plate of eggs, bacon, and bread in front of me. Butter and jams are soon pulled from another bag. Picking up a jeweled fork he placed beside the plate, I dig in.

To his credit, Lassar does try and sit in the other chair. It's comical the size difference. His large body causes the delicately crafted chair to whine with each shift. With a sigh, he forgoes the chair and sits on the ground. From that height, he's more level with the table anyways.

I can't help but smile.

"Thank you," I say softly. Lassar's eyes find mine. "Not just for the food. For the clothes...and for everything else."

The dragon's smile is equally as soft.

"You had nothing, Anwyn. I couldn't let you set off unprepared. The journey is dangerous enough."

"Still," I say, "thank you. You didn't have to do all of this."

"I did, Anwyn." His voice is so earnest it makes something warm bloom in my chest. My heart, cold and iced over from years of solitude, feels like it's beginning to thaw in this warm cave.

"You're welcome, all the same." His smile is wide, showing me his sharp teeth. "For the clothes and the food... and everything else."

I giggle into my breakfast plate.

He really is a kind dragon, and I am beginning to feel bad for my earlier thoughts of killing him. If I'm being honest with myself, this is the best I've been treated by anyone in a long time. Not saying much for humankind. This dragon may care for me because he wants my body, but he's been respectful toward me.

Though, I wouldn't mind a few more orgasms before I left. I've lived a lonely life. What can I say? The pleasure he gave me is a thousand times better than what I've been able to do with my own hand.

My chest feels funny again as I look toward the mouth of the cave. The pounding of rain and the claps of thunder sound ominous in this quiet cave.

"That storm sounds terrible," I venture. Lassar nods, eating the last bit of his bacon between two claws before licking them clean. I wouldn't mind knowing what that forked tongue feels like on my pussy, either.

Maybe I've truly lost my mind in this cave, but I can't bring myself to care.

"It's a strong one," Lassar agrees.

With a sigh, I turn towards him. His eyes are so bright they warm my face. I don't break his stare as I ask the next part before I lose my resolve.

"I was wondering if you wouldn't mind, of course, if I could stay here. Just a little longer until the storm passes." I let out a laugh and shrug. "I'd hate to get all the nice dresses and shoes you bought me ruined with mud."

"You can stay as long as you want, my Anwyn." His smile is as bright as his eyes. "When the storm clears, I can fly you to where you want to go. If that sounds alright to you?"

My heart pounds in my chest as I nod. The warmth in my chest spreading down my arms, into my stomach, and dancing along my fingertips.

"That sounds perfect."

THE STORM DOESN'T LET up for three days.

Each one of those days became more precious to me than the jewels littered around this lair. They were each nothing but pure, peaceful bliss. Passing so quickly that when I woke this morning with Lassar's strong body next to mine and did not hear the usual pounding of the rain, a deep sadness clogged my throat.

We had settled into a comfortable routine. Lassar cooks me a delicious breakfast each morning, and then we will explore the cave. He found me a drawing pad, and I will sketch for a few hours. I'm not very good, but Lassar says I show great talent. My sweet, lying dragon.

In the evenings, he will leave to get more supplies, and he no longer chains me up. We spend our nights talking. Sharing stories, mostly from his past. The life he lived as a mortal man. When we first met, he was so animalistic, but now he's almost human again. Well, as human as someone who breathes fire can be.

I don't do much sharing, and Lassar doesn't press me. Mostly, I'm just content with being in his presence. That is more than evident each night when we go to sleep on the floor together. Lassar wraps himself around me, my spine molded to his chest. The first night was strange, but it didn't take long for me to settle.

He hasn't touched me like he did the first night, and I haven't asked him to. I desire his touches, but the longer I've spent in his company, I realize I desire him as well. He's protective of me, caring, and kind. Not since I was a child have I felt this relaxed and looked after. Lassar always makes sure I have exactly what I need. Some would find his attentiveness stifling, but I crave it.

Like now, as he sets down another hot plate of eggs and bacon, sadness takes hold of me as I realize I may never find this attentiveness again if I leave. A human man could never do this, provide for me in this way. Lassar covets me like a treasure in a way only a dragon could.

We eat in silence for a moment as my new feelings war inside me. Lassar seems to be aware of the shift in weather as he picks around the food on his plate.

"The storm seems to have passed," I say softly, my stomach curdling. I am hungry, but I can't bring myself to eat.

Lassar's eyes find mine, and he nods. The loneliness that has been gone from them for the past three days swims in his gaze once more. From the tales he's told me, he is truly alone in this world. Just like me. No one from his past life is alive anymore.

"I should probably get going," I say into the silence. It feels like a mistake to leave. Where will I get comfort like this again? Is my independence worth forsaking this? Having the means to live alone and my own freedom has been the one thing I've craved for so long.

Lassar has me questioning if it would really be so bad to belong to someone else.

My dragon nods his head and collects my plate. I go to the leather bags and begin stuffing them with the items Lassar got me. My eyes burn as I secure the tops. This feels wrong, so incredibly wrong.

When I stand and turn, Lassar is right behind me. Making me gasp. His large hand comes up to my face, gently rubbing his claws over my cheeks. The look in his eyes is devastatingly soft.

"I wanted to thank you," he says, his voice deep with emotion.

"For what?" I ask; surely I should be the one thanking him. Look at all he's done for me.

"For showing me what it's like to be a man again, for making me remember how wonderful life can be. Over the years, this curse has taken much from me. There was a time when I could barely remember anything beyond my desire for more gold. But no longer." He leans in, pressing his lips against my forehead. Tears leak down my cheeks.

"Getting to know you, my precious Anwyn, was the greatest treasure I have ever found. No gold or jewel or silk could ever compare to you," he says into my hair. With one last kiss to my forehead, he steps back and turns, walking towards the mouth of the cave.

"Lassar, wait!" I shout, his whole body freezing.

Perhaps it's reckless, foolish, or any number of unsavory words, but I don't care. I can't let this end here, not yet.

I do some quick math and speak to Lassar's scaled-back.

"I arrived here four days ago," I say. Lassar slowly turns, nodding his head.

"That means it's the end of the working week." Lassar's brows lower, and inclines his head, clearly not knowing where I'm going. Truthfully, I barely know what's coming out of my mouth at this point. "Finding lodging at the next town might be difficult, as well as getting work on the weekends. Perhaps it would be best if you took me to town at the start of this upcoming week?"

Lassar blinks once, then twice before smiling. The sight makes my heart pound.

"I can take you in two days from now, my Anwyn."

I sigh at the use of *my Anwyn*. It's rare he calls me anything but his: his precious one, his treasure, his Anwyn. I find I rather like his names for me.

Letting my leather bag drop to the floor, I look at Lassar expectantly.

"Since I'm not leaving, what should we do?"

Lassar looks to his right, down a passageway of the cave we have yet to explore together. Raising his hand towards me, I walk forward and take it. His large hand engulfs mine, the scales rubbing against a few callouses I have on my palms. Lassar had lamented at those, saying someone with hands as delicate as mine shouldn't have been forced to work.

I was in total agreement with that.

"There's something I've been wanting to show you. Come."

He leads me deep into the bowels of the cave. The deeper we get, the darker it becomes until the rocks around us are illuminated in faint blue light. I've seen them before, Lassar explained they are some rock formation that glows. It helps guide us along our path until we reach an opening.

I gasp at what I see there. A large pool with still, clear water. The entire thing comprised of those glowing rocks illuminating the water.

Dropping his hand, I venture to the side of the pool. Dipping a finger in, I yelp at the freezing temperature. Lassar lets out a small laugh behind me and then comes to my side. With a deep inhale, he produces a mass of scorching flames. Their heat makes my eyes water. It's not long until the pool is bubbling and steaming, heated by his fire.

"I thought you might like to bathe."

Nodding my head, I can't think of anything better. It's been days since I've bathed, and while I don't think Lassar minds, I certainly do. I watch my dragon pull out a bar of soap and a few hair-cleaning tonics I've only seen in fancy homes.

"From the trader, he said these are the best for fine hair. Your beautiful hair, my Anwyn, deserves only the best."

I blush and nod, lifting the wool dress over my head. I'm standing in only my shift, the humid air causing it to stick to my skin. Lassar looks down at me and growls before quickly turning away.

"I'll leave you to it."

Letting him go would give me an opportunity to think. To be sure this is the decision I truly want to make. But each click of his claws along the stone floor feels like a knife in my heart. It sounds ridiculous, but I've already let this dragon give me an orgasm with his tail.

My sanity has clearly left a long time ago.

"Lassar!" I call. He turns back towards me, and with

confident hands, I pull my shift off of my shoulders and let it pool at my feet. Lassar's golden eyes take in every inch of me. His tongue licks over his lips like I want it to lick over me. I see the outline of his cock pressing against his leather pants. My pussy is already turning wet and slippery.

With a small smile on my lips, I meet his stare.

"Bathe with me."

8

LASSAR

Anwyn's golden hair is plastered down her naked back as she hangs onto the pool's edge.

I'm happy my beautiful Anwyn likes this place. I knew she would. I hadn't let myself hope that she'd allow me in here with her. Not yet, at least, but she had. Now my gaze is hungry as it takes in her bare skin. My cock pushes against the front of my leather trousers I still have on as I recall what she looked like, completely naked.

Small breasts and small hips. Her nipples were the same perfect pink as her lips. Her little pussy was hiding beneath a dusting of blonde hair between her thighs. My mouth waters again at the memory. I could eat her whole, but she's not mine yet.

Even though she agreed to stay longer, she still plans to go.

Not yet. I still have time to make her mine, to prove to her that I am worthy. If she doesn't choose me, I'll spend my life following her from the shadows, ensuring she is always safe and cared for.

I should be caring for her right now.

As if my thoughts reached her, Anwyn turns towards me. Her opal eyes peer over one delicate shoulder. The side of her breast is just visible as both hands are curled beneath her head at the pool's edge. I glide towards her in the water, droplets clinging to my scales.

My precious Anwyn smiles. She picks up the hair tonic next to her and holds it out to me.

"Would you mind washing my hair, Lassar?"

Without a word, I move quickly, snatching up the glass bottles and dumping the contents on her hair and my hands. The lavender and citrus scent fills the space around us. My claws dig into her scalp, scratching and massaging lightly as I clean her silken hair. Even wet, still sparkles in the lowlight. It is a privilege to tend to her like this.

I tell her so.

She moans as I continue to work the tonic into a lather.

"No one has washed my hair since my mother when I was a girl." My claws slide down to her neck, gently rubbing away the tension there too. Anwyn is quiet about her past, but I am as greedy as ever to know more about her. To covet each new piece of information about her like it's a rare jewel.

"Can I ask about your mother?"

Anwyn nods. "She was beautiful and kind. From what I remember, at least, she passed when I was ten. My father loved her so much that he died from a broken heart a year later. At least that's what the town told me." I shrug, emotions clogging my throat. "I barely remember anything from that time."

"And you've been on your own? Since you were ten?"

"Yes. I stayed with a farmer and his family for a few years, but they had too many mouths to feed, and I didn't want to become a burden." Her voice has so much sadness that I can't help but slide closer to her. Letting my wet scales press against her smooth skin, she takes a deep breath. My head comes down on top of hers, and she leans back against me, the round cheeks of her ass cushioning my cock.

I swallow down a hiss as Anwyn continues.

"I moved around from town to town after that. Always on guard, always looking for a new opportunity to exploit. I've seen the worst of people and done things I'm ashamed of to survive."

"You did what you had to," I say, rubbing my claws through her hair again. Anwyn is quiet as I rinse the tonic from her hair. When the suds are gone, she glances over her should at me again, a small smile on her plump lips.

"It's odd that a dragon was the one who made me have faith in humanity again. I've been so relaxed here I feel like my old self."

I suppress the urge to puff out my chest. I've pleased my precious one, I feel like a king.

"I'll always take care of you, Anwyn. Even if you choose to leave, I'll always make sure you're safe." She smiles at me again. Her smooth back is still in front of me, and I gently drape her long hair over her shoulder, exposing the expanse of it. Taking the bar of soap, I rub it along her skin until it's soapy. Using my hands, I work out the stiff muscles in her back.

Anwyn moans, tilting her head to the side.

"I'm ashamed of the man I used to be. How could I have been so selfish and arrogant? Consumed by my own greed as to enter into a bargain with a demon and to be cursed to live in this monstrous form." My hands press more firmly into a particularly tight muscle. "I thought it was a death sentence, and in some ways it was. But now..."

My hands still on her back, emotions weighing down on me.

"But now what?" Anwyn asks, her opal eyes curious.

"But now, I think it was a blessing. As I said, I never would've met you otherwise, and if by some chance we had when I was human, I wouldn't have been worthy of you. My greed would've blinded me to the treasure you truly are. Now, like this, I see what you are, who you are to me. And I must protect you with everything that I am. This curse has given me the power to do so, and for that alone, I will be grateful to the demon I once hated."

I rinse the soap off her back. Anwyn is quiet for a few moments until she turns from the edge. Treading water, her beautiful breasts are bared towards me. Her hard nipples skim the top of the water, her eyes gazing into mine. She's so gorgeous I have to look away, her body too decadent for these monstrous eyes.

"Lassar," she calls gently. Her hand finds mine in the water, wrapping around my wrist. My head turns back towards her; her eyes are darker than I've ever seen them. They could lure me to my death, and I'd go willingly. "Lassar, touch me. Please."

A need to claim pounds in my veins, but I am gentle with my precious Anwyn as I grip her around the hips and set her on the edge of the pool. She gasps as her warm skin meets the cool stone floor. She bites her lip, her hands going to my shoulders. With her like this, we are almost the same height.

My claws skim up her sides before cupping her breasts. She arches back as her own hands explore my body. I memorize every detail of my treasure, from the freckle on the side of her left breast to the faded scar on her right shoulder. Letting my tongue slip from my mouth, I lick over the raised skin, and she shivers.

She is delicious. I can't believe she's letting me touch her like this.

Anwyn's hands skim over my chest, tickling my scales there. Her fingers dip into my back muscles, pulling me closer to her.

"You're so warm, Lassar. It's like there's fire in your blood." Her thighs open, releasing the sweetest scent from her cunt. She's wet, I can smell it. I'm desperate for a taste. Her legs wrap around my waist, the heat of her pussy cradles my cock through my pants, and my control snaps. The feeling of her wet flesh unleashes the monster inside of me.

"Can I kiss you, my precious Anwyn?" My hold on my beast is breaking, but I will not fail her now. Not when she has shown me this trust. I need to hear my precious one say that she wants me.

Her smile is mischievous, her cheeks rosy from the warm water.

"Only if you promise to do a lot more than just kiss me."

I growl, the sound echoing around us.

"Be sure of what you ask me, my precious one. I've been holding myself back for days. I don't want to scare you with the depth of my desire for you."

The thought of her being frightened of me makes my stomach turn. Anwyn merely smiles wider. Her hands trace down my chest again, down the hard plane of my stomach until they reach the lacing of my trousers. With one small finger, she runs along my bulging cock.

My breathing is coming in pants as she tilts her mouth up, her lips dancing over mine.

"I wouldn't ask for it if I wasn't sure I could take it. All of it."

With a broken groan, I slam my mouth on hers. She opens for me like a flower; her moans are like honey on my tongue. My claws rake over her, kneading her breasts, skimming down her back, and grabbing her ass. She moans for me, wrapping her arms around my neck to pull me in closer. Her little cunt continues to rub against me.

I drag the scales on my chest against her nipples, and she gasps, her greedy pussy soaking me with more sweetness. Grabbing her ass harder, I pull her even tighter against me. My tongue slips into her mouth, tasting her fully. It tangles with her smaller one, gentle at first. Then I'm feasting on her. I break the kiss to focus my attention on her neck.

My tongue skims up the side of it as she grinds against me.

"Your pussy is so wet, my Anwyn. Is it wet for me? For the dragon who caught you?"

Anwyn sighs, her head lulling back. Something about me reminding her how I got her makes her work her hips faster against me. My hand slips down to her soaking wet pussy. Her flesh is warm and soft as I run a claw through her slit.

"Well? Tell me, Anwyn. Tell me why you are so wet."

"You," she pants. "You made me ache like this. Now you need to take care of it."

I smile against her neck. Take care of it, I will. I will be the only one who serves this sweet pussy. If any man or creature even dared to smell her, I'd kill them. Scorch their corpses. The monster inside me agrees.

Gliding my finger through her folds, I work her clit in

tight circles. Her muscles go tight, and her mouth opens as she looks at me. Her opal eyes are hazy, lost in pleasure.

"I'll soothe you, my precious one. I know just what you need."

"Please," she begs.

My tail comes out of the water and gently pushes at her shoulders, urging her to lay back on the stone floor. The blue lights around us cast her wet body in the most beautiful glow. Like this, she is a feast I plan on devouring.

But I need my Anwyn to know what this means. If I have her this way, no one else ever will.

"Are you going to let me lick your cunt, my Anwyn?" She nods her head furiously.

"I'll be the only one who's ever tasted you, isn't that right?" Again she nods, too consumed with the need to come to answer. "No one else will ever see your pussy. Or I'd have to kill them. Wicksome wanted you, wanted my treasure, and I killed him. I'd do it to anyone who covets what's mine. Do you understand, my precious one? You are mine. Mine to keep, mine to protect, mine to fuck."

"Yes," she says. "I only want you. Taste me. I ache for you."

"I want you to soak my face. Cover it in your come." I lean down, smiling against her wet flesh. "Then I'm going to make you lick it off of me."

Anwyn screams as my tongue parts her folds. Her cunt is so pink and pretty, glistening in the glowing lights. Using my hands, I gently pull her folds apart to see all of her. I run my tongue from her asshole to her clit, and she squirms.

Holding her open like this, I spit into her entrance, watching the saliva pool there. Soon my seed will run out of this hole, but not yet. Tucking my claw just inside her,

Anwyn moans. My blood is on fire, rushing in my veins as her cunt grips my finger.

"You're so tight, my precious one. Going to have to go slow at first, but you'll take my cock, won't you? I'll just have to make sure my Anwyn is soaking wet first." I laugh as more of her arousal soaks my hand. "That shouldn't be a problem. You're soaking me now."

"Lassar, please, stop playing with me."

I can't help it. When it comes to Anwyn, I need her so worked up, delirious in her need for me, that I consume all her thoughts. That she knows I'm the only one who can satisfy her like this. She likes it too. I can tell that by the arousal seeping out of her little pussy.

I breathe on her heated skin, her calves coming to rest on my shoulders.

"Do you remember when you told me all you knew of dragons was their perchance for stealing princess?"

"Y–y—yes."

"In all of the stories, did you ever read what happens when a dragon captures a princess he has no wish to return?"

"N—no. I don't think those would make very good children's tales."

I laugh against her, licking her clit with the broad side of my tongue.

"They wouldn't." My tongue licks over her pussy again. "You said you weren't a princess, my Anwyn, but I don't think that's true. Your pussy is sweeter than any wine and worth more than a million golden bars. Kings would wage war over you, and I will lay siege to anyone who dares come for you."

"Lassar," she moans, her hard nipples thrusting into the air.

"This dragon has caught you, and he's keeping you." I stare deep into her glassy eyes. "Now let's see if you come like a princess."

My tongue glides over her, sucking on her clit while simultaneously dipping into her entrance. Her hands cup her breasts, but I push them away and replace them with my own, rolling her nipple between my fingers. Her body grows tighter, more delicious nectar leaks from her, and I'm eager to lap it all up.

"Lassar, it's too much. I'm going to—I can't—"

"You're going to take it. You have no choice, I own you. When I want to lick your cunt until you pass out from pleasure, I will." I growl against her, the vibrations causing her hips to rise. "When I want to fuck you, spill my seed deep inside you until you swell with my child I will."

Children were something I mourned, along with my humanity. But the thought of Anwyn, swollen with my child, has me feasting on her cunt with more vigor.

"Lassar, I'm—"

"I think there are better uses for your mouth, my precious one."

I slip my tail up her chin, pushing it past her lips. Her mouth is warm and wet as she closes her lips around the tip of my tail. Thrusting it in and out of her mouth like I would my cock, Anwyn licks and sucks. Her mouth makes obscenely sloppy sounds. Sliding it down her throat bit by bit until I bump the back of it. My precious one coughs, her eyes watering as I retreat. Spit dribbles out of her mouth and coats my tail.

Her teeth gently graze my tail, sending a shiver down my spine. I have to will myself not to come in my pants, but my control is shattering.

"Naughty girl," I admonish. Sucking her clit into my

mouth once more, I slip a finger into her entrance. My head spins at the perfect tightness of her. The way her cunt strangles one finger and then a second. Hooking them inside her gently, I fuck her with them. Careful not to go too deep. The barrier of her virginity will only be broken on my cock.

She grinds her hips against my hand, fucking herself on my fingers. All the while, her hands hold onto my tail, pumping it in and out of her small mouth. My Anwyn was perfect before, but now...there are no words.

Her body goes tight, and she's close to coming, I know just the thing that will send her over. Pulling my tail from her mouth, I slip it down her body. My fingers pump her, and my mouth works her clit. With one slight nudge, my tail slips past the tight ring of muscle of her ass, and Anwyn screams.

The sound echoes around us as she shakes through her orgasm. Her back arches clean off the floor, her legs trembling on my shoulder. There are red marks all over her from my claws, teeth, and scales, and I growl with possessiveness.

Her come flows out of her, covering my chin as I rush to catch all of it in my tongue. Anwyn grabs my face and grinds herself against it, her clit bumping up against my nose. Once I've licked every drop, I pull back, watching her small body shaking with aftershocks.

"You don't come like a princess," I say, trailing kisses up her chest and neck. "You come like my naughty human captive. A dirty little girl who spreads her legs for the dragon who caught her."

Anwyn blushes.

"I'm only naughty for you," she says in a soft voice. I laugh and kiss her lips, sharing her taste with her.

"I suppose I should forgive my naughty girl?" She nods her head.

"Please, I'll be good."

"How are you going to do that?" My hand cups her pussy, which is already growing wet again.

"By keeping my promise." Her soft pink tongue licks up my chin and lips. Licking me clean of her come, just like I told her she would. My Anwyn, a gift I don't deserve.

I cup her cheek, enjoying the high of playing these games but needing to make sure she's alright.

"Are you well? Do you need anything?"

She shakes her head but then shivers. Scooping her up, I carry her body back toward my lair. Quickly, I get the fire going as I lay her down in the pallet of silk and pillows. She spreads out on the sheet like a queen. Her eyes calling me back to her.

"Are you hungry? Thirsty?" I ask, kneeling beside her. "I'll make you some food."

Anwyn grabs my arm before I can stand.

"The only thing I need right now is you." I never thought I'd hear those words from her lips. A broken groan escapes me.

Anwyn guides me between her legs again. I am careful not to give her my full weight. Her hand trails down my stomach and unlaces the fly of my leather pants. It's not long before her curious hand is holding my cock, stroking it. I growl into her neck, pumping my hips into her fist.

I don't need to see her to know she's smiling as she whispers, "My turn."

9

ANWYN

Lassar is everywhere as I hold him in my hand. His claws skim over every inch of my naked skin. Just like in the pool, the sensation causes goosebumps to break out along my body. What he did to me then lit a fire inside of me. I've never experienced the type of pleasure I felt at the hands of my dragon. No human man could do what he did to me. I know that in my heart.

The silk beneath me is cool against my hot skin.

His mouth consumes mine. Over and over, his lips press into mine. They're scaled texture is rough, while his forked tongue is soft as it tangles with mine. He tastes like fire, smoky and heady and I want to drown in it. I give his cock a tentative stroke. I've never done anything like this, but I know human men are not this well-endowed. Or covered in soft ridges that mimic the scales on his body.

I shiver as Lassar lets out a groan.

"Does my cock please you, my Anwyn?" he asks. I nod my head. "Say it."

"Your cock pleases me, Lassar," I pant, his mouth sucking on my neck, biting the skin gently.

"Pleases you enough that you're going to open your pretty thighs for me? Going to let me fill you with every inch of it? Even if it's a tight fit?" His claws knead my breasts as my hand continues to explore his shaft. Our mingling growls and moans echo around us in the lair.

"Even if it hurts, Lassar," I say, meeting his eyes.

"You're so perfect, my Anwyn. My most precious treasure. Now that I've found you, I'll never let you go. I'll have claimed you forever once I fill you with my seed." His tongue licks over my ear, causing me to shiver. "I already own your pussy. Now I'm going to own your heart."

Lassar gives my earlobe a gentle bite before kissing down my neck again. He's not wrong. Something changed between us while we were at the pool. It should frighten me, but it doesn't. I can't live a solitary life anymore, now that I know Lassar exists. I thought I wanted independence, but I don't, I want to be owned. Kept and cared for by the dragon whose claw is running through the wetness pooled between my legs.

I'll let him own me, but I want to own him too.

His mouth returns to mine, and we are a flurry of teeth and tongues again. My hand slips from his pants and helps shove the garment down. We break the kiss as I get my first glimpse of his cock in the dim light of the cave. My mouth goes dry.

Feeling it was one thing, but seeing it is quite another. It's the same green shade as the rest of his body. It hangs heavy between us, a bead of white moisture already at the tip. I want to taste it, to feel those ridges against my tongue.

Lassar did say he'd always give me what I need. Right now, I need his cock in my mouth.

I nudge his shoulders, and Lassar pulls me with him as he lies on his back. His wings have spread out behind him on the silk sheet. My naked front fits along his scaled body. I marvel at our size difference, my head resting under his chin while my toes barely graze his knees. Sliding up his body, I press a soft kiss to his lips, his yellow eyes wide as I grip his cock in my hand.

"My precious one," he groans as I tug on him, running my palm along the soft scales of his shaft.

"Yes, my dragon?" I smile as I kiss him again. He makes me feel powerful. Who knew being captured could be so freeing?

Lassar's tongue licks over my lips. More of his come seeps onto my hand and the soft skin of my stomach where his cock is trapped between us. Over and over, I pump him until he is thrusting into my hand. Even his wings grow tight at my movements.

"You are too perfect, my Anwyn. I don't deserve you."

My cheeks heat, and my pussy turns even wetter. I jerk him one more time before shuffling down his body. Kissing each scaled muscle as I go until I get to his monstrous cock.

"I've never," he pants, "I've never laid with a woman in this form."

"Good," I say, licking up the wetness at the tip of his cock. His taste explodes along my tongue, and I instantly want more. "We'll be each other's first time."

"Each other's only time," Lassar growls, his tail skimming up the inside of my thighs. He wants a declaration from me. And I will give him one soon. For now, I take his cock fully into my mouth as an answer.

Slowly, I drag my tongue along his shaft, gliding over the rough texture. His skin is warm and salty and all mine. Saliva leaks from my mouth and coats his length. Pulling my mouth from him for a moment, I spit into my hand and use it to pump him as I wrap my lips around him once more. Lassar's claws fist my hair as his growls swirl around us.

"Pretty, pretty, Anwyn. How beautiful you look with your mouth around my cock." I moan around him, the vibrations causing him to groan again. "I'm going to fuck your mouth like it's your pussy. Going to come down your throat and watch you swallow it."

I moan again, and this time I feel something glide along my pussy. The blunt head of Lassar's tail nudges my fold, gently caressing my clit. I double my efforts, sucking him deeper into my mouth until he nudges the back of my throat. My eyes water, and I cough, but that only adds to the slickness. My hand and mouth work him together as his hips thrust into my mouth.

"This is what you wanted, my Anwyn. This is what brought you to my cave. You knew I'd give you the fucking that you need. First your throat and then your pussy." His hands tighten on my head, pulling it up to meet his eyes. "It won't take long for you to let me have your ass either, my precious one."

Before I register what's happening, his tail slips into my ass. It pushes gently passed the tight ring of muscle, and I squeal. The sensation is overwhelming and perfect and something I want to experience for the rest of my life. I'm close to coming, and I need Lassar with me.

Pulling my mouth from his cock, I jerk him roughly in my hand as his tail slides in and out of my ass. Our eyes lock, and I bite my lip, the tip of his cock inches from my lips.

"Come in my mouth, Lassar. Come all over me, I want to be covered in your seed. I need it." With one more harsh tug, I smile. "And then I want you to fuck me so hard I won't be able to move afterward. I want to lay in front of the fire while your seed leaks out of me from everywhere."

Lassar groans, his abs tightening, and I know he's coming. His tail pushes deeper into my ass, and my body locks up. Flames lick up my skin as my muscles tighten. All I can do is suction my mouth to his cock and swallow down his release while my body shakes through my climax.

I swallow and swallow until it leaks from the sides of my mouth down my chin. Pulling back, I make sure Lassar is watching as I lick my lips, tasting every bit of him. He groans, his eyes heating as a few more splashes of come paint my breasts.

My arousal coats my thighs as I crawl up his body, straddling his stomach as I kiss him. His claws rake over my body, squeezing my ass. Our kiss is slow and tender and full of emotion. My body is tired, but I don't want to stop. I need him, all of him.

"Are you alright, my Anwyn? Sleepy?" I simply shake my head at his question.

"I'm ready for more," I say, resting my elbows on his chest.

"More?" He curls a lock of hair around one claw. A few of the strands tangle in his scales. I place a kiss on his chest and nod before sliding off of him and laying out on the silk blanket. My skin is sweaty and sticky from his release. Lassar can wash me later. Right now I need to have him inside me.

Spreading my legs for him, he crawls towards me and settles between them.

"Anwyn—"

"I want you inside me." I bite my lip and curl my arms around his neck. "More than that, I want to give myself to you. I'm your treasure, right?"

"Yes," he growls immediately.

"Then I want you to enjoy your treasure fully. You have full control over me, do with me what you want."

Lassar's eyes darken as he stares down at me. It's a dark desire, one I'd never give to another but Lassar. He won't hurt me, I truly believe that. I've always had to be the one with a plan, making decisions. Having someone who I can give my body, my heart, my trust and know that he won't abuse that power? It's heady and what I've just given to my dragon.

"Anwyn, you trust me? I've finally earned your trust?"

"Yes," I say, pulling him down for a kiss. "Now own me."

Lassar snarls. His claws scoop me up and hold me to his chest. My hard nipples rub against his scales. As does my pussy, covering him in my arousal. I can't get enough. My body craves the connection. Lassar's tongue licks over my ear, his hot breath tickling me.

"Do whatever I want with you, my sweet Anwyn. You have no idea what you're asking for." His claws skim up my sides and circle around my back. "But I'm going to show you."

Lassar stomps us over to the stalactite on the floor. The golden shackles are still hanging from them. It wasn't that long ago I was contemplating his death while attached to them. Now, as he locks both my wrists to them again above my head, I realize I'm going to let him fuck me in them.

A delicious shiver runs through me.

Lassar sits back on his heels, his tail flicking wildly, as he takes in the long expanse of my naked body. With my arms bound like this, I can't touch him. I'm completely at his mercy, just like I wanted. I don't feel scared giving him this control. A part of me, a part I never knew existed, settles at the thought of being owned by him fully.

"Look at you, my precious one." His claws graze down my chest, circling around one nipple. "Laid out before me like a feast. Your sopping wet pussy is begging for my cock."

"Please, Lassar," I whine.

"Shh," he says, squeezing my breast before leaning down and licking my hard nipple. "When I'm done with you, Anwyn, there won't be a single piece of you I don't own. Look around you, look at all the treasure I've hoarded, and know this. I would sell it all—burn it all—to keep you."

I moan as his other claw goes to my pussy, gently rubbing my clit. The shackles clink as I flex my hands, desperate to hold on to something.

"I scare everyone in this cursed form. But I don't scare you, Anwyn. Your pink cunt is soaking my hand, demanding I fuck it." His finger enters me in shallow thrusts. The sloppy wet sounds of my arousal cause my thighs to clench. "I'll be fucking it every day for the rest of your life. It doesn't matter if you leave to live a normal life, I'll find you. Burn your home down and fuck you in the ashes. Do you understand?"

I cry out as he slips another finger inside of me. Lassar's never spoken to me like this, and it should scare me. It has the opposite effect as I feel my arousal coating the inside of my thighs. I want what he's saying, I want to know that if I did leave, he would come for me and bring me back here. That I truly do belong to him.

"Y—yes!" I shout as his fingers continue to pump me over and over again. Lassar slides between my thighs as he pulls his fingers from me. I watch through heavy lids as he grips his massive cock in his hands and rubs it through my wetness. I sigh as he drags those ridges along my clit.

"You're mine, precious one. Mine, say it." The head of his cock pushes into me, and my body tenses. I already feel full, and he's barely inside me. My hands tangle in the gold chains.

"Say it, Anwyn," Lassar demands again, giving me another few inches before retreating. My legs curl around his hips, holding me tightly to him. Lassar rears back to give me another few inches.

"Say i—"

"I'm yours!" I cry, raising my hips to meet his thrust and sealing him fully inside me. There's a pinch of pain from being stretched so wide. Lassar doesn't move, only breathes hard as he stares down at me. My own chest is rising and falling in time with my wild heartbeat. His hand cups my cheek, his claw pushing into my mouth where I suck the tip of it.

Lassar groans, slipping his hand down my throat and collaring me there. His touch is light but controlling all the same. I love it.

"You don't know how beautiful you look like this. My claw around your throat; your tight little pussy wrapped around my cock." Lassar gives my throat a gentle squeeze. "Are you alright, my precious one? Is my cock too much for you?"

I shake my head, the pain stopping and a deep desire for my dragon to fuck me like he promised.

"I need more, Lassar. I need you to fuck my pussy, to own me, I'll die without it."

It's euphoric, not just the feeling of being stretched by him but to be able to admit my desires to him. This dragon owns me, and I want him to enjoy every bit of it as much as I know I will.

"My beautiful Anwyn wants me to fuck her?" Lassar's hips pull back before he slams back into me. My breasts bounce in time with his thrust. "The little human who stumbled into my cave now opens her legs for me. Begs me to ravage her pretty cunt and fill it with my seed."

Lassar fucks me even harder. His hands hold up my hips to get an even deeper angle. The soft scales of his cock graze my inside walls, the sensation making my toes curl. My mouth hangs open as I moan with each delicious thrust.

"There's no mention of dragons fucking the human princess they capture in your stories, Anwyn. We can make our own story." His tongue slips out of his mouth and licks over each of my nipples. "They'll tell our story in every town. The human girl on the run and the dragon who captured her. Every day he provides for her, kills all those who would come for her, and at night she thanks him with her beautiful pussy. Letting him use it and fill it over and over until she grows round with his child."

I groan, my hands yanking hard against the shackles. I'm surprised they don't rip from the stone.

"That's your legacy Anwyn. To live as the dragon's pampered fucktoy. His ultimate treasure. That's what you want, isn't it?"

"Yes! I want it!"

"I'll always give you what you want." His lips come down on mine, and our tongues tangle as he powers into me over and over. My body tightens, and my thighs begin to quiver. His thrusts turn more frantic. I feel his tail glide through the cheeks of my ass before pressing into me there.

That's all it takes, the sensation of him filling both my holes at once as my climax barreling into me. My body erupts into flames as my heart pounds in my chest. I scream his name into the cave, the sound echoing throughout. My pussy clamps down on his cock as if it knows what's coming next.

Lassar is quick to follow, his body freezing before he

gives me one more thrust. His hot seed fills me, leaking out from my pussy and sliding down towards my ass. My dragon fucks it into me, making sure I have every drop.

"My precious Anwyn, my beautiful Anwyn. Tell me you're mine for as long as I can have you. Tell me your mine for eternity," he murmurs, pressing kisses to my open mouth.

Reaching up, he unshackles my wrists, my arms falling limp to my sides. My whole body is trembling. Lassar holds me to his chest, carrying me over to the pallet on the floor. He doesn't set me on it. He keeps me in his arms, his chin resting on top of my head.

His request still lingers between us. There's so much that I want to tell him, but my body is exhausted. In the morning, I'll share everything that's in my heart, but right now, I just need him to hold me. My whole world has changed in this cave, and I don't fear it.

As my eyelids close, I'm able to slur one last word before the darkness consumes me.

"Forever."

10

ANWYN

These past two days have gone by in a blur. Since the first time Lassar took me, it has been a nonstop cycle of fucking. The comfortable routine we had before has changed slightly. Now, every morning he wakes me with his head between my legs, his tail gently pushing into my entrance or my ass, depending on his mood. He makes me come with his tongue and then with his cock, pushing into me and fucking me while my screams echo through the cave.

Then he feeds me breakfast before we return to bed. Sometimes he will shackle me or tie my hands with silk fabric and make me ride him. We don't stop until we're both exhausted, and my stomach growls. Lassar then cooks me a filling meal before we start touching each other again. It's not long before I'm on my back, and he's inside of me, filling me with more of his seed.

As I lay in the silk sheets now, his come from last night is still drying on me. This morning is different as I pat the sheet next to me and don't find my dragon. Perhaps he has gone to get more food? Our supplies were dwindling last night, and he couldn't pull himself away from me long enough to get any more.

The thought makes me smile. As absurd as all of this is, I can't deny the truth. I'm falling in love with a dragon. He makes sure I'm safe and cared for. He fucks me without mercy. Lassar is everything I need, but more importantly, he's everything I want. I've been meaning for us to have a conversation, but there hasn't been much time for talking.

When he gets back, I'll make time for it, I want him to know how I feel.

Stretching my arms above my head, I realize just how sore I am. Every muscle aches, and there is a dull throb between my legs. I need another bath, but I don't want to wash Lassar from my skin. Each time he fucks me, he makes sure I'm soaked with him. I remember his words from our first time together about making me round with his child. My hand rests on my stomach.

We haven't taken any precautions. Could I really get pregnant by a dragon? What would that even look like? I can't say that the thought doesn't appeal to me. I missed out on my family, I would love to be able to have my own with Lassar.

I'm due to get my courses in the next week. If they come, then I'll start on the contraceptive herb, and if they don't, I guess Lassar will have to share me sooner than he antici-pated. A giggle bursts from my lips as I flop back down on the silk sheets.

It's quiet outside the cave, sunlight filtering in between a few of the rocks. Maybe Lassar and I can explore *The Woods* together today. Fuck outside for a change.

Movement sounds at the mouth of the cave, and the sound of Lassar's claws along the stone floor has my pussy heating. I'm addicted to him. I push up onto my elbows and watch him enter into the lair. His eyes find mine, and I smile, but his face remains serious.

Looking at the bags in his hands, my brows furrow. One is filled with supplies, while the other is empty. Lassar looks at the floor, his shoulder hunching.

"This bag will be able to hold a substantial amount of gold coins. Enough to buy a house should you need it. I got you some new dresses as well, in case if you end up somewhere warmer, the wool of the others will be too thick."

My heart pounds in my chest.

"Am I going somewhere?" Lassar's shoulders grow tighter at my question.

"The weather is mild today, perfect for flying. My offer to take you where you want to go next still stands."

My mouth falls open. Oh, my sweet dragon, how can he think I'd want to leave him? We hadn't discussed my staying outside of the declarations given during our lovemaking. What I said then stands now. I'm staying with him forever.

I'll just have to show him that I mean it.

Rising from the floor, I let the silk sheet fall from my naked body. Lassar's eyes lift from the ground and take in my body. My hard nipples, my thighs still coated in his come, and my wet pussy that is begging for his attention. I pad over to him. His chest rises and falls. His wings spread out behind him.

When I'm right in front of him, I push onto my toes and kiss his mouth.

"I'm not going anywhere, Lassar. I'm staying here with you forever."

Lassar growls, his hands gripping my head. Our kiss deepens, his rich flavor exploding in my mouth. Our tongues tangle together. He walks me backward but I stop him. I want him to fuck me, but not yet. I want to show him that I meant every word I just said.

Sinking to my knees before him, I undo the lacings of his leather pants.

"You've given me everything I could ever need. Let me show you how much I want to be owned by you." I groan as his cock springs free. Reaching behind me, I grip an over-stuffed pillow and kneel on top of it. To cushion my knees but also to give me some height and position his cock right at my lips. There's a bead of come at the tip that I lick off.

"My precious girl. You. Are. Mine." Lassar growls each word.

"Yours," I agree before taking him fully into my mouth. My tongue glides along his soft scales. My hand pumps him into my mouth. His length bumps the back of my throat as his claws cradle my head. I bob up and down on his cock, saliva coating him. His hands tighten in my hair.

"My Anwyn sucks my cock like she was born to do it. Were you, precious one?"

"Yes." The word is muffled with his cock still half down my throat.

I work him over and over again. His hips moved in time with my mouth. He grabs fistfuls of my hair to hold me steady as he fucks my mouth. Mercilessly until I'm gagging, my eyes water in response.

"This throat is mine, I'll fuck it how I want, and you'll take it. Until I slip down your tight little throat."

I nod my head as he continues to pump into me.

"I'm going to come, Anwyn. Keep your eyes open. I want you to see what you do to me." I keep my eyes wide as I watch Lassar lose control above me. His movements become sloppy until his body locks up, and he spills down my throat. I swallow his seed, loving the taste of it before he pulls himself from my lips and coats my breasts with his come. It's warm as it lands on my skin.

Running my finger through it on my chest, I lick it clean as we lock eyes.

"I love that you were willing to let me go, Lassar if that was still what I wanted to do. That's why I'm yours. You're the only one who's ever cared this much about me. Ever wanted ~~to~~ me this much. I love that, I crave it. Almost as much as I love you."

Lassar's eyes go wide, his whole body ridged. He doesn't say anything for a moment. I wait for his reply as he stomps off. My brows lower as I watch him dig through a pile of gold. The coins hit the stone floor with soft clinks before he returns back over to me.

He crouches down before me to show me what he's collected. It's a simple gold band. My eyes water as he holds it out to me.

"My precious Anwyn, I was a cursed creature before I found you. I thought I would spend forever miserable and greedy. Now that's all changed. I have you, my Anwyn, and you require this form in order for me to keep you safe. You are my human captive, my most precious treasure." Lassar snags my hand and slips the ring on my left hand. "You are my wife, I declare it to be so. You are my everything Anwyn, just like I am yours."

My laugh is water as I loop my arms around his neck. It's unorthodox, it's strange, but I've never lived a normal life. This is perfect. Lassar is everything to me. I don't see the future as uncertain or something I'll have to navigate my way through. My future is with Lassar, and it's filled with love and happiness.

Our mouths meet, and Lassar lifts me. He carries me and sets me back down on the silk sheets. He settles me on my back, but I smile, gently pushing at his shoulders. Lassar obliges me, and I crawl in front of him. He growls as I walk on all fours and thrust my ass out towards him.

He loves having me on my hands and knees. My dragon moves behind me, his claws holding me firmly by the waist. I look over my shoulder and watch his fork tongue slip from his mouth. Lassar buries his face into me from behind. He licks my clit and my entrance with broad strokes of his tongue.

Over and over, he licks me until I'm moaning, my hands fist the sheets below me. His tongue slips out from my entrance and licks my asshole, dipping just inside. It's decadent and obscene. It's wrong, but the pleasure is too good.

"I'll fuck this little hole soon enough." Lassar's claws spread my cheeks open, his tongue licking me over and over again. My pussy is so wet my arousal is running down my thighs. Lassar's claws return to my hips and hoist me up.

He gives no warning before he plunges inside of me. My back arches as I moan. He's so deep this way, the scales of his cock sliding along my inner walls until I'm panting. Like this, he's able to hit a spot deep inside me, making my toes curl. His clawed hand smacks down on my ass, and I feel heat bloom there. His tail slips between us to rub my clit. It's too much. It always is from this angle.

Now slick with my arousal, his tail slithers down to my ass. I cry out as it begins to enter me there. The stretch from his tail and his cock feel like I'm being split in half. I don't dare tell him to stop.

"Look at you. Both of your holes being filled—"

There's a noise from the mouth of the cave that has both of us freezing. Lassar stops pumping into me as the sounds get closer. It's voices. At least a dozen different ones. Lassar's hands snag my waist as he snarls. One voice is clearer than the others. My mouth opens when I recognize who it belongs to.

Mrs. Hitherbend.

"Dragon!" she yells. "We know you killed Mr. Wicksome and have the girl. Let her go, and there will be no trouble."

Lassar growls again.

"Stay here, my precious one. I'll deal with whoever has dared to enter our cave."

Lassar moves to pull out of me, but I reach back, holding him still. I don't want violence to come to these people. I'm sure my dragon won't think twice about burning their bodies. Mrs. Hitherbend was kind to me in her own way. I don't want her to meet the same fate as that evil Wicksome.

"Don't stop fucking me just because they're here," I say, encouraging him to move within me once more.

"But Anwyn, I need to make you safe. I—"

"Oh, dear gods!" Mrs. Hitherbend cries as she enters the lair. The ten people from the village she brought with her also pause in shock. One could think it was because of all the immense wealth right in front of their eyes. However, something tells me their shock is coming from seeing me being mounted by a massive green dragon.

"Let her go, you foul creature!" A few of the townspeople point pitchforks and torches at Lassar. He snarls at them, but I grip his hand on my waist. My eyes meet Mrs. Hitherbend as I shake my head.

Lassar begins to move inside of me, and the townsfolk gasp in horror.

"Sweet child, we've come to save you from this beast. Look at how he defiles her!" she shrieks towards the townspeople. "I went to that doctor you told me about, and he's helped me remember things. I know you aren't my sister's, but I can't let you be this creature's plaything."

"I chose this," I moan as Lassar hits that deep spot inside of me again. His claw wraps around the back of my neck, holding me down as he pounds in and out of me. My body is fully covered by the sheet and the pillows, but the scene before them is clear.

"You should be happy for me, Mrs. Hitherbend. I did what you said," I pant as Lassar doubles his efforts. His tail moves at the same punishing rhythm in my ass. Our skin slapping together echoes around the townspeople. "I found a man I love to take care of me."

"Child, this beast—"

"Has taken her from all of you. She is mine," Lassar growls, his tail plunging in even deeper into my ass, making me moan. "Look at how she screams for me. Hear how wet her pussy is. She loves this, loves being owned by this beast. Tell them, my Anwyn."

"Yes! I love it, I need it." His hand smacks my ass again.

"She's so hungry for my cock, I wake in the middle of the night to find her slipping me inside of her. Insatiable, my little human." I moan. It's true I need him all the time. "I wear myself out in this little cunt every day. Just like I will for the rest of our lives. You can't take her from me. She's mine."

I should be appalled at the words he's saying, but I find myself craving more of them. I want them to know he owns me. This is what they need to hear, so they'll never come looking for me again. I never want to see another person beyond Lassar for the rest of my life. He's all I need, and I'm ready to seal my fate.

"My dragon, I'm close. Come inside me, I need more of your seed."

Mrs. Hitherbend looks pale, as do the townsfolk around her. Lassar's hand on my neck pushes me down onto the floor. I'm completely helpless as he ruts into me at a punishing pace. I feel him breathe in deeply before the smell of fire permeates the air.

I look up in time to see the flames he's roared at the townspeople. Not enough to hurt them but enough to have them scurrying away.

"Leave and never come back, Anwyn is mine!"

My body tightens, both my holes clamping around his cock and tail. His clawed hand slips to my throat and pulls me up, his tongue running along my spine.

"No one but me gets to watch you come," he growls.

"Forever?" I ask.

"Forever." I'm helpless to do anything but obey. My body is awash in pleasure as he fills me to the brim with more seed.

EPILOGUE

5 Years Later - Lassar

My beautiful wife is being naughty.

Does she think I can't smell her sweet scent on the wind as I soar above the trees? I returned to our cottage only moments ago, expecting to find her just as I left her. Relaxing in our bed where I could feed her before fucking her again like I had this morning. She prefers to stay indoors when I have to venture into town.

I typically travel into town under the cover of night with a dark hood in order to prevent giving the sellers there such a fright. However, my Anwyn has been craving oranges, and the trader who sells them was only passing through town today. I slipped him a little extra coin, and my scaly skin and claws were soon forgotten.

Those oranges now sit abandoned in our cottage while I search for my wife. We left the cave a few months after our mating. Anwyn had gotten her courses and decided to start taking the contraceptive herbs. While getting her pregnant would've been a joy, it just wasn't the right time for us.

Instead, we decided to move deeper into *The Woods*. Somewhere remote but close enough to a town for me to get the things my Anwyn needs. Those early months were heady. I barely left her thighs long enough to feed her. Our love is less frenzied now but nonetheless all-consuming. Recently it's been ramping up again at Anwyn's insistence, and I will never deny her pleasure. Each moment we spend together, we somehow sink deeper into our feelings for each other.

Every day that I've spent with Anwyn, she has become more and more beautiful. My gold helped us buy the supplies for the cottage and will keep us and whatever children we may have in the future comfortable for the rest of our lives.

This curse has given me the perfect life, and I never thought I'd ever be grateful for it. But I am.

I growl as I see a flash of blue from below. Swooping down, I swallow a snarl as I see the blue dress Anwyn was wearing earlier hanging from a tree. We are deep in the woods as I begin my descent toward my wife. There is a meadow bursting with all types of beautifully colored flowers off to the side. They all pale in comparison to the beauty of my precious one.

She is oblivious to my approach, completely naked and spread out atop a silk blanket. Even though I've tasted every inch of her skin, and been inside her countless times, when I see her like this, it's just like seeing her for the first time.

Silently, I creep up beside her. Moving quickly, I cover her mouth and pin her to the ground. The setting sun illuminates her golden hair, making it blend into the silk sheet. Her opal eyes are wide with surprise as she screams into my hand. It's not long before they lower, joy replacing the surprise.

"I've caught you, my precious one. The dragon has you now. No ransom will be enough for me to give you back." Anwyn moans into my hand. I slip between her thighs, her pussy soaking through my leather pants to tease my cock. She's so perfect. It's a mystery she's real.

Anwyn raises her hips to drag her pink cunt along my cock, needing the friction. She loves this game we play. Her the helpless captive, and me the dragon who's come to claim her. It's because she knows that she holds all the power between us. I live for her, I breathe for her, and that's how I gained her trust, and with it, her surrender. A loud ripping sound cuts through the air as I shred the fabric she's resting on with my claws. I quickly use it to bind Anwyn's wrists and hoist them above her head.

Her naked body is laid out for me to use however I want. I press a soft kiss to her lips.

"Lassar," she moans as I break it.

"What was your plan, precious one? Did you think you could really escape me?"

She shakes her head, her breasts jiggling with the movement.

"The evening was lovely, I just came out here to enjoy it."

"You mean you wanted to show your body off to anyone who saw you. Wanted to let them catch a glimpse of your pussy." My claws close over her wet flesh. "My pussy. Did you think I would allow that?"

Anwyn smiles softly, my claws parting her folds and rubbing her clit.

"I don't care who sees. But you're the only one who gets to touch."

My blood heats as I look into her beautiful face. She

always knows exactly what to say to have my cock painfully hard. Leaning down, I run my tongue from her pussy, up her stomach, over each hard nipple, and then along her neck.

"That's right. I'm the only one who gets to have you forever. Let me make sure you remember that," I whisper against her ear.

Without warning, I plunge two fingers into her wet cunt. Her arousal coats my hand and allows me to get nice and deep, scissoring them within her until her back is arching. Her beautiful breasts are thrust into the air as I claim a nipple.

"Even after all these years as my captive, your cunt still begs for my touch." I pump her a few more times before pulling them from her entrance and dragging them lower. I slip one finger into her ass as she squeals and thrashes in her restraints. "This hole welcomes me just as much, doesn't it?"

"Yes! You own them," Anwyn pants.

I've only taken her here with my cock a few times. She's so tight in her little ass I can barely last a few thrusts. Tonight, I'll use my tail. When we're back in our bed, I'll make her grip the footboard as I also push into this hole.

"Beg me to fuck you. Show me the treasure I got when I captured you."

Anwyn's cheeks are pink, but she's a good girl. Her thighs spread wide on either side of me. Pressing up on her heels, she presents her wet cunt to me. It glistens in the setting sun, her scent strong and sweet on the wind.

"Fuck me, Lassar. Fill me with your come. Use me however you want. You own every inch of me."

With a roar, I rear back and push my cock inside her tight pussy. She's slick and hot and grips me tight enough to make my teeth clench. That storm that sent her into my cave was a gift. A chance to prove that I had learned from my past life. That there was more to life than gold and greed. There's Anwyn. Every thrust inside of her body is more precious than a million gold coins.

The greatest treasures in this world are priceless, just like my Anwyn.

My tail slips beneath her to press into her ass. She loves being filled like this. Her thighs tremble where they're locked around my hips. Bracing both clawed hands under her thighs, I push them up and back to expose her to my eyes fully. Her wet pink skin looks perfect, being stretched by my cock and tail.

Anwyn's eyes are clouded with lust, and I know she isn't going to last much longer.

"Say it, Anwyn." I spit down on her pussy, watching the saliva catch around my cock. "Say it, and I'll make you come."

"I love my dragon! Make me come, please."

My claws pinch her clit, and she's done for. Her little cunt locks around me, milking every ounce of my seed that I'm more than happy to spill inside of her. My spine locks as I pump her full of my come. It splashes between us, covering both of our thighs. I love making a mess of her. She loves it too.

Reaching up, I gently slice through the tie on her wrist and cuddle her against me.

"How are you, my precious one?" I ask, tucking some hair behind her ear.

"Perfect, I love when we play our game," she sighs, cupping my cheek. She nods towards the meadow beside us. "We should take some of those flowers back to the cottage. They'd really brighten up the sitting room."

Glancing behind me, I shake my head.

"Those belong to the Faerie King. Anyone who takes from his meadow must serve him in his court below *The Woods* for eternity." My arms tighten around her.

"Too bad I'm already serving someone else." She winks at me as I press a kiss on her forehead. Gently, she takes my hand and holds it to her stomach. "Though, you might have to get used to the idea of sharing me."

My heart stops. Anwyn's cheeks are rosy as she smiles up at me. The setting sun paints her in gold. This may be the most beautiful she has ever looked. I register what she is saying, and now it all makes sense. The cravings, how insatiable she's been to fuck lately. My grip on her flat stomach tightens.

"I've missed my last two courses," she says softly.

"You're pregnant?" I place a kiss on her stomach as she nods.

"Are you happy?" she asks.

"Yes. This means we're going to be a family."

"I know," she says, her eyes rimmed with tears. "It's something we've both wanted for so long. I can't believe it's finally happened."

"I love you, my Anwyn. My precious, precious wife. My life was nothing before you. You've given me everything."

"I love you, Lassar. You take such good care of me, I know that you'll love our child just as much." Anwyn's mouth presses against mine. A cursed dragon lord and an orphaned human. Brought together by chance. With the evidence of our love now growing inside my Anwyn. This life is perfect, something gold could never buy.

Anwyn kisses me hard, rolling me onto my back as she climbs on top of me. My cock is instantly hard again as she braces her hands on my chest. My hands hold her hips as she rubs her clit along the scales of my stomach.

"What do you say we give that old Faerie King a good show?"

My hands on her hips tighten as she grips my cock and rubs it along her wet slit. Both of our come leak out of her and allows the head of my cock to slip inside her easily.

"I'll always give you what you need, my wife."

Anwyn sinks fully down onto my length, her moan loud enough to send the birds scattering from the trees around us. I raise my hips, meeting her thrust for thrust. Over and over again.

The life we built together lays out before us, worth more than any amount of gold.

ACKNOWLEDGMENTS

Big thank you to my beta readers for their feedback on this novella! This one took me awhile to rot but Anwyn and Lassar's story is one that I absolutely love. Make sure you've read A Kiss From a Demon to meet the one who cursed Lassar into his monstrous form. Lots of projects are the way from me. Make sure you're following me on Instagram & TikTok so you never miss anything.

Another massive thank you to Haya, from @hayaindesigns on Instagram for my cover! Who's ready for a sexy Faerie King and the human who accidentally takes from his meadow?

ALSO BY CHARLOTTE SWAN

Subscribe to my newsletter for all the latest updates on upcoming projects!

Monstrous Mates Series

Available on Kindle Unlimited

Taken by the Dark Elf King

Captured by the Orc General

ABOUT THE AUTHOR

Charlotte Swan is a twenty-four-year-old, living in Chicago. When she is not dreaming about being whisked away to a world filled with magic and sexy monsters, she is busy being a freelance social media marketer and full-time smut lover. To read her debut novel *Taken by the Dark Elf King*, hear about her upcoming projects, or to connect with her on social media please find her on her website or by scanning the code below.

www.authorcharlotteswan.com

Made in United States
North Haven, CT
06 August 2023

40027300R00064